I0556222

The Desolate Trail

A Novel by
Clifton LaBree

© 2015 by Author, Clifton LaBree

Published by
Fading Shadows Imprint
New Boston, New Hampshire, USA

ISBN-10: 1-943329-19-2
ISBN-13: 978-1-943329-19-9

Cover Design by Vivian LaBree

Dedicated to my wife Pauline, and my family, with thanks for all their support and encouragement.

Chapter One

October 22, 1781

Colonel Levi Wilson leaned his rifled flintlock carbine against a white pine tree and wearily sat down to rest. A strong, cool wind swept across the water, blowing his long gray hair. It felt good against his face. There was a hint of winter that would soon descend upon the northern wilderness. He looked across Lake Ontario with a squint in his eyes, watching the sun fade behind the western mountains. The large fort behind him at the mouth of the Niagara River protected the portage from Lake Erie to the Niagara. Over the years, it had been the scene of fierce battles since its construction by the French. The promontory was alive with the ghosts of dead British, French, American, and Indian soldiers.

Colonel Wilson and a small group of his scouts had escorted a tribe of Delaware and Wyandot Indians, on the verge of starvation, into the sanctuary of the British-held fortification under a flag of truce. The fort had become a destination for many displaced Indians threatened with extinction and starvation. Their request for food and sustenance severely taxed the limited resources of the garrison troops. Yet, they were quick to honor Levi's entrance into the compound and had treated him and his men as honored guests instead of enemy agents.

A courier rider had just ridden into the fort to notify the garrison that the British had been defeated and had surrendered at Yorktown, Virginia. The news instantly triggered speculation about the final outcome of the brutal war that had about drained the resources of the original colonies to sustain it. Every man and woman in the fort grew silent and

1

reflective, wondering if the courier was correct. Confidence in the reliability of news was a scarce commodity, so there was a "wait and see" attitude in the air. Most prayed that it was true. Levi had absorbed the news and felt the need to be alone. He closed his eyes, thankful for the veil of darkness that hid the tears rolling down his weather-beaten face into his speckled gray and black beard. If the news was correct, then it meant that they would soon be able to go home. The thought of home conjured up memories of dead men and women who had defended the pursuit of liberty. The physical, emotional, and monetary sacrifices for the cause were shared by their families, who had suffered even more.

Levi had been a major player in many of the conflicts leading up to this crucial moment. He never forgot the long, treacherous trails he had followed in the pursuit of justice, or the heroic men who had fought at his side and were now gone. They had died in lonely, desolate wilderness landscapes mourned and remembered by few. History would never acknowledge their individual acts of bravery or their dedication. Without their collective sacrifice, victory would simply be a wondrous dream, never a reality. It was those special few who died alone, frequently under savage circumstances of bestiality, that Levi could never forget. His tears were in their honor. He was saddened to think that when he, too, met his Maker, there would be no one left to mourn their contribution to civilizing the wilderness. That fact bothered him because they had left a legacy of courage and commitment worthy of recognition and emulation, even though courage and virtue are their own monument and reward.

Lieutenant Angus Campbell, one of Levi's officers, exited the large mess hall building at the fort, looking for Colonel Wilson. It was getting dark, and he was impatient.

"Guard," he snapped at the nearby sentry. "Have you seen Colonel Wilson?"

"The last I saw of him, he was heading towards the lower town by the river, Lieutenant. I wouldn't be surprised if he was sitting in that stand of pine on the edge of the bluff. It's a quiet spot to sort things out."

Campbell curtly acknowledged the sentry and took off towards the pines at a dead run. "Colonel Wilson, where are you?"

Wilson heard the young officer and shook his head, wondering what crisis demanded his attention. "I'm over here, Angus."

"We've just received a message from General John Stark at Albany," Campbell informed the Colonel, taking a seat on the ground next to him. "Evidently the Northern Department has no more monies or supplies to distribute to the militia forces. That means no pay for our efforts again. He knows, maybe even more than us, that the northern frontier is still a dangerous place. Criminals and enemy elements, especially Tories, are still running at will throughout the countryside, killing, stealing, burning, and terrorizing the inhabitants."

Colonel Wilson sighed and replied, "Nothing has changed in that respect, Angus. The lawlessness on the frontier is more of a civil problem than a military one. Pretty soon old man winter will impose a temporary truce upon the land. We should return to our homes in New Hampshire for the winter months and try to recruit the assistance necessary to enforce law and order in the Grants come next spring. We may have time to help process firewood and hunt some game before the heavy snows settle in for the winter. Prepare the men for an early withdrawal come morning."

He thought about the small settlements of New Boston, Starktown, and Derryfield in central New Hampshire when he was a young man. They had been on the edge of the frontier. The sparsely settled communities were subject to frequent attacks by Indians designed to capture people for ransom, a lucrative enterprise for the Abenaki at Saint Francis. The isolated settlers were constantly vigilant for a surprise attack by the dread Abenaki.

"You're right, Colonel," Angus turned to study the ruggedly built frontiersman with the sad eyes, noting his private anguish and penetrating stare, searching the distant horizon. Campbell had known this strong gentle man since he was a small boy; yet, he was never able to anticipate what Wilson was thinking. "Well, Sir, I'll leave you to your thoughts. I've never told you how grateful we have been for your loyal and courageous service. I've considered it a privilege to serve with you. God knows that you've earned the right to a warm hearth and a long overdue rest from the rigors of combat. I wish you well, Colonel."

"I appreciate that, Angus," Levi replied in a soft voice. "I've traveled a lot of trails over the years. The one I like the best always leads to my home in New Boston."

Left alone again, Levi closed his eyes and leaned his head against the white pine tree, reliving the echoes and images from a past that still haunted him. It had all started in Rutland, Massachusetts, four years before Levi was born, when his dearest friend, Phineas Stevens, whom he had loved like a brother, was a young man. If he remembered correctly, it had been in July of 1722.

* * *

Sixteen-year-old Phineas Stevens slowly walked toward the meadow where his father had been harvesting hay all morning. Accompanied by his three younger brothers, Phin, as he was affectionately called, was joking and laughing with his siblings as they anticipated the hearty lunch they were bringing to their father who had been laboring all morning in the hot sun mowing swamp hay. The sturdy oak pail was filled with venison stew and biscuits. The aroma from the container whetted their appetites, for it had been six hours since they had eaten breakfast of oatmeal sprinkled with dried apple slices and maple syrup.

The youngest Stevens boy, Mark, was four years old. He was content to ride on his big brother's shoulders where he could see better. He played a game that made all of them laugh. Without warning he would clasp his hands over Phin's eyes, and Phin would make believe he was running into a tree ready to spill Mark off his perch. Finally, Phin protested that if Mark continued with his game, he might have to walk. Mark got the message and gently hugged him around the neck, whispering, "I'll be good, Phin."

Their mother had harshly warned them that they must maintain vigilance and stay close to each other, ever on the alert for the feared Penobscot Abenaki Indians that frequently raided isolated homesteads in the frontier regions of the New

Hampshire Grants. There was a continuous battle for survival against the infamous raiders from their village located north at the junction of the Saint Francis River and the Saint Lawrence River. Vicious massacres and unspeakable butchery had been taking place against the settlers on a regular basis as they pressed north and west into traditional Abenaki tribal lands.

The conflict between England and France for control of an empire inevitably involved the native population, who generally sided with the French, using their influence to inflame and incite the Indians to new levels of savagery. Most blamed the black-robed Jesuit priests who cajoled, bribed and indoctrinated their flocks to kill and destroy the English. Some priests accompanied the raiding parties and led them into battle like a pack of mad dogs, vigorously urging them to greater levels of inhumanity against their enemies.

The northern frontier had been in flames for several generations. Competing ideologies of the opponents were a large part of the problem. The French had come to the New World to make their fortunes on furs and timber with the hope of returning to Europe with their fortunes. The British came to the continent, lured by the prospect of owning land that they could work and reap the fruits of their labor. They had severed roots from their land of birth to begin a new life. Their concept of property ownership was the main issue of contention with their Indian neighbors who believed that the land, sky, water, and animals belonged to the Great Spirit and could not be sold or bartered.

Land ownership was at the heart of the conflict that ensued after the settlers began to clear land on the frontier. Settlers displaced the Indians from their ancestral lands, even though most homesteaders believed that they had rightfully purchased the land from the original owners. Deception, theft and trickery was involved in many of the land transactions, which did nothing but incite a vicious struggle for survival. The strongest and fittest being the victors.

The Stevens family had purchased a tract of land in western Massachusetts about thirty miles east of the Connecticut River. Vigilance was a way of life on the frontier. A nearby family, mother, father, and two children, had recently been killed early one morning by a small band of Abenaki. The

Indian leader had cut out the father's heart and eaten a portion of it, because the father had courageously defended his family. The Indian was paying tribute to the man's valor, but the settlers were abhorred by the barbarity of the act.

Phin and his brothers were within seeing distance of their father who was diligently mowing the hay. They paused at a small stream to get a drink of water, when five Indians leaped from the cover of alder bushes beside the stream. They quickly encircled the brothers, silently killing two children. Phin was just taking Mark from his shoulders and had a firm grip on his arms when the Indians struck. Frightened at what he had just witnessed, Phin grasped Mark to his chest to protect him, too scared to even scream to his father. Phin tried to run away only to be clubbed beside the head, knocking him and Mark to the ground. His two brothers' bodies were floating in the bloody water, making him sick to his stomach, and more frightened than he had ever been in his life. The image of their wanton murder and mutilation would stay with him forever.

One of the Indians tried to wrench Mark from his grasp, but Phin stubbornly refused to let him go, continuing to shield him from the blows aimed at both of them. For some reason the Indians stopped and silently pushed him and Mark into the forest out of view of his father, forcing Phin to run with them toward the west. Clinging to Mark with a desperate determination to protect his little brother, Phin began to retch. The image of his brothers being beaten to death and left in the bloody pool of water was more than he could stand. He paused to empty his stomach and to his surprise, the Indians also stopped.

The small band had attacked, murdered, and scalped two innocent children who were not a threat to them, and escaped before Phin's father and uncle became aware of the gruesome deed. The column continued to run at a trot for several miles. Phin was running on adrenalin, his leg muscles ached, and his arms were weary hanging on to little Mark.

He was a strong, ruggedly built young man with an articulate and modest mannerism inherited from his mother who had taught him to read and write, and, most of all, she had introduced him to poetry and literature of all types. The family made every effort to include as many books as possible in their small family library at the modest log cabin in the Massachusetts wilderness. Few families could read and write or afford such luxuries, but Phin's parents saw their children's education as an important part of their growth to responsible adults in a new land filled with opportunities that their native Scotland severely lacked.

Carving a living out of a wilderness required long days of hard work, clearing the land of rocks and tree stumps to make room for the crops the family needed to survive the long, cold winters. For the first few years, Phin was adept at girdling tall trees to kill them, making room for the sun to penetrate between the standing boles where they scraped the soil and planted corn, squash, pumpkins, and gourds. Later, they would cut down the trees for firewood and remove the stump. In time, they created large fields for growing crops, a testament to the grueling hours of sweat and hard work. Phin had proved a good worker, and was always ready to do his share of the labor.

The column of Indians and their two captives wound through the wilderness for several miles before they stopped at a hilltop location for a rest. A small swampy area was visible from their location where they spotted a doe deer feeding in the open. Two warriors left the group to approach the animal from opposite sides. The remaining warriors warned Phin and Mark to remain quiet and motionless. Earlier on the trail, Phin had been quite successful in keeping Mark quiet, but without warning, a small branch he was unable to deflect as the person before him had brushed past it, hit Mark in the eyes, and he cried out. The child's outburst drew a strong reaction from the Indians. One instantly grasped him around the mouth to silence him. With much gesturing and deadly threats, they warned Phin to keep him quiet, or they would kill him on the spot.

Frightened by their rapid response, Phin tried to show them he would keep his brother quiet and spoke softly in Mark's ear, "Listen, Mark. If you don't be quiet, they're going to hurt you, and there would be nothing I can do to prevent that. Please, hang onto me and duck your head so as to not be slapped by branches again. Do you understand?"

Little Mark accurately perceived that his outburst had placed both of them in grave danger. "I'll be good, Phin."

A short time later, the two hunters returned triumphantly carrying the deer. A fire was started with dry wood, and they all ate their fill of fresh venison roasted over the small, hot flame. Once hunger was satisfied, they cut the balance of the deer meat into strips and quickly seared it for preservation over a longer period of time than raw meat.

Towards the end of their first day, they stopped to make camp for the evening on the eastern shore of the Connecticut River. Phin was exhausted from carrying his brother and keeping up with the speed of his capturers. The Indians paid more attention to Mark than to Phin. They seemed amused at how well he obeyed his big brother's orders. One offered to carry Mark for a while, but Phin refused to give him up.

Half of the group had left to fish the river and returned with two large brook trout. Phin helped them to clean the fish and cook it. The trout was a welcome change from the venison strips, and the fire felt good to Phin and Mark as the sun began to set. They were given two deerskins for the night. Phin laid one on the ground with the fur side up and placed the other one over him and Mark who curled up against his big brother. They slept the sound sleep of the exhausted in a fetal position.

In the morning, they were brusquely awoken and directed to three canoes hidden in a swampy lagoon beside the river. The captives were placed in the center of the largest canoe with an Indian in front and the rear. The light canoes were quickly pushed into the stream while several Indians looked at their back trail with anxious frowns. Their concern gave Phin some hope that his father and uncle might have been on their trail, but his hope faded as they entered the Connecticut and headed north upstream at a rapid pace.

The canoe ride was welcomed by Phin, who was still aching all over from his previous day's exertions. It gave him a chance to recover from the ordeal and to consider what was ahead for him and Mark. He had carefully listened to his parents and visitors when they talked about the Indians. The French Jesuit-led Abenaki in Canada retained all of their native fierceness and were encouraged to use the tomahawk against the enemies and perceived enemies of the Catholic Church as determined by the fanatical group of Jesuit priests. Their conduct was in contrast to that of the Moravian missionaries from Germany, in particular a very popular minister, Reverend Frederick Post, who became a noble spokesman for the native population of North America. The Moravians labored diligently to create apostles of peace and for the Indians to disavow their war-like tendencies and ferocious instincts.

Completely bewildered about where he and Mark were being taken, Phin took careful note of specific landmark features as they passed through them. They traveled up the river for an hour and crossed over to the western shore, following a slightly worn portage trail on a westerly track for less than a mile to a small creek. The Indians stopped for a rest after carrying the canoes over the trail to the creek. Here they hurriedly ate some of their deer meat and then pushed off into the small stream. At this point, the Indians warned Phin to have Mark lie motionless at the bottom of the canoe, and for him to be careful not to puncture the fragile birch bark skin covering the light craft. They also indicated to Phin that they did not want to take a chance that Mark might fall overboard in the deep water and drown.

They traveled for a day near the center of the stream with the Indians paddling as quickly as possible. It was evident that they were anxious to get out of the confining and potentially dangerous position of being attacked from either side of the creek. At the end of the day, they had made it to the southern end of a larger body of water Phin correctly anticipated to be Lake Champlain. Once they started up that large lake, Phin's hope for rescue was rapidly dashed. The frightening and vast wilderness was swallowing them without a trace.

Chapter Two

Phineas and Mark Stevens slept that evening on the southern shore of Lake Champlain. The next morning they ate their fill of fresh water salmon the Indians had caught the night before.

The size of the lake fascinated them. It was sunny, and they could see large mountain chains on both sides of the lake. Phin knew that they were traveling a northerly route into the heart of Abenaki country. The wilderness was so vast, and they were so small and insignificant. Concerned and apprehensive about the future, Phin still was able to admire the beauty of the landscape. The mountains in the west were a brilliant blue with the sun focusing on them.

The two captives were rushed into the canoes as soon as they had finished eating, and their trek to the north continued. They spent two days on the lake, hugging the eastern shore. They were forcefully reminded to remain still and to be careful of the bark bottom of the canoe. Once they had to stop and repair a leak in one of the canoes when it grazed a rock and opened up one of the seams. It was early in the summer, and the growing season was at its peak. They quickly located a large white birch tree nearby, easily removing a three-foot-wide piece of bark, fastening the bark to the existing structure with pitch from a balsam fir tree which they had with them in a small gourd.

Early on the third day, their journey over the water ended. They had entered a large bay and landed on the northern shore. At this point, the Indians became much friendlier toward their captives and relaxed, joking amongst themselves. They tried to tell Phin that they were on their way to St. Francis River and up to their village called Odanak. Phin understood the name of the village, for his family had often said that most of the Indians that roamed the northern frontier were from that place.

Odanak had become the center of resistance to English expansion. Various native tribes from Northern New England such as the Pennacooks, Sokokis and Cowasucks had freely roamed the area for generations. The Abenaki, *People of the Dawn*, were the dominant group of native tribes. The French had established a Catholic Church at the encampment for their vigorous missionary campaign. At the time that Phin and his brother were taken captive, there were about 700 members in the village.

The Indians, settlers, and land speculators all had different visions for the future. Each vision depended on acquiring or retaining land occupied or desired by other people. This variation of dreams and visions was at the heart of the bloody conflict that lasted so long on the northern frontier. The contest for a homeland would yield in favor of the strongest and most powerful contender, but until that was settled, many tears and much blood was shed by all parties.

The two white boys became objects of interest to members of the village and were treated fairly. Some even treated them with respect and affection. Their captors had told the people how well disciplined they had been on the long trip to the village. The people respected those traits of character. They also admired the way Phineas strenuously protected and cared for his little brother. Those were manly traits they also admired. He had the potential of becoming a fine warrior, and several were considering adopting them into the tribe. Others argued, just as vehemently, that the two would bring good gifts from the white man if they were ransomed. They were in good condition and would bring a top price. The tribal council agreed to an exchange. They were thus advertised as if they were a commodity for sale.

The exchange came later in the summer after their demand was made known to the white community. Two representatives, one from New Hampshire and the other from Massachusetts, came to the village under a white flag of truce to consummate the exchange. The tall, slender individual from Massachusetts was Reverend Frederick Post, a well-known Moravian missionary. Phineas and Mark were traded for two chests filled with copper cooking pots, blankets and $100.00 in

11

gold coin. Reverend Post successfully argued that the two prisoners should be sent back home with a supply of food for the trip. The party left mounted on horses amidst shouts and waves from the village people. Reverend Post remained behind at the village.

Phin's experience as a captive was a memorable milestone for the rest of his life. It tempered his evaluation and judgment of the Indian community. He understood that they were the original occupants of the land and that they had been treated unfairly by the newcomers. He admired many things about their culture and way of life. However, their tendency toward cruel and inhuman treatment of their enemies perpetrated a long-standing distaste which he took to his grave.

He settled into a life on the frontier at Rutland and worked his acres and began to raise a large family. Self-educated and intelligent, Phineas became a natural leader among his peers in the frontier community. His strong, athletic physique was honed to perfection from long hours cultivating crops and cutting firewood to feed the ravenous appetite of the fireplace in his cabin.

The conflict known as the King James War erupted on the northern frontier in 1743. It was the beginning of a different life for Phineas Stevens who was known as a wily frontiersman with leadership qualities that were scarce on the sparsely settled area of New England. The Abenaki of St. Francis, with a justifiable reputation for savagery, spread throughout New England, bringing devastation and death to unsuspecting settlers in isolated cabins and clearings. They torched homes, scalped men, women, and children, and brought more frightened captives to Odanak for ransom.

The French Jesuits began their conversion of the Abenaki. The so-called "heathen" people admired the Jesuits for their stoic courage and ability to live with the native people. Thus, they followed their teachings and were eager communicants to Christianity. The Jesuits taught them that the heretic English had crucified Jesus Christ, and thereafter, the Indian's vengeance for real or imagined wrongs added to the motivation for the terror flowing across the borderlands.

The Governor of New Hampshire, Benning Wentworth, and Governor Shirley of Massachusetts were concerned about the inflamed frontier. In early October of 1743, they ordered a fort to be constructed on the east side of the Connecticut River at the settlement of Charlestown. The fort was named Fort Number Four because Charlestown was the fourth settlement at the northern edge of the frontier. It would provide protection for the settlers in the region against French and Indian depredations, which were almost a daily occurrence. Those closest to the structure would benefit the most, but all of the borderland region would find a certain level of security in its construction. It was, at the least, a stabilizing factor on an otherwise unprotected wilderness.

Governor Wentworth also commissioned Phineas Stevens as a Lieutenant in the foot company of militia volunteers. The small band of militia included men from New Boston, Amherst, Londonderry, Starktown, and Rumford, a hardy group of men who knew first-hand the extent of the troubles on the northern frontier. One of the men who joined the militia was Levi Wilson of New Boston. That fall, Phineas assembled the volunteers at the site of Fort Number Four to review their tactics, line of supply, and organization for the campaign the coming spring when the snows melted. They discussed ways they could best defend the borderlands. Several inches of snow had already covered the ground. Teamsters were busy dragging pine logs and hardwood firewood into the construction site of the fort.

Levi Wilson arrived at the rendezvous mounted on one of his faithful Narragansett horses. Shorter and less muscular than Phineas, Levi had a reputation of being a hard worker with notable endurance and tenacity, capable of carrying out long journeys either on foot or horseback. His mild mannerism and decisive intelligence was respected as much as his fleetness of foot, but his gentle demeanor was his most admired characteristic. He had a special affection for the Narragansett horse breed. They possessed a gentle disposition and the heart of a lion, working well in the forested wilderness with their surefootedness and relatively small size.

Phineas turned to Levi Wilson with a serious look. "I'm glad to have you in our group, Levi. We're in for a difficult time this spring. There isn't much we can do with winter at our doors now, but we can use the time to plan ahead. Would you accept the rank of ensign as second in command of the company?"

Levi was feeding his horse a handful of oats. He knew Phineas from previous gatherings on this same subject. They had served several times together on the trail of Indian raiders. "I'll take the responsibility, Phineas. I've been thinking a lot about how we can utilize the company of volunteers. If we patrol in large numbers we'll be able to defend ourselves better, but we'll be limited in the amount of territory we can cover."

"What are you suggesting, Levi?"

"Well, I think we could provide better protection for the inhabitants of the borderland if we were a mounted company split up in groups of three or four men each. We could then cover a greater amount of territory and gather more information by avoiding direct confrontations with the Indians. If we stand off and observe their movements and report back to a central control group, say on a daily basis, then we would have a fairly accurate picture of what's taking place on the frontier. That way, settlers who are the most threatened could be forewarned to seek protection."

Phineas smiled at the proposal. It was what he would have expected from the serious and studious Levi. "Your suggestion makes sense, Levi. Mounted patrols could cover more area, and the horses would give them an opportunity to avoid a fight unless it was impossible to do so. My only thought is that the horses would leave a much more discernible trail than a man on foot."

"Therein lies another value with the mounted patrols, Phineas. The known presence of mounted scouts could act as a deterrent. The most terrifying and successful tactic used by the Abenaki is stealth, a surprise attack on an unsuspecting forest dweller. Mounted patrols, if vigorously prosecuted, could remove some of their surprise. We could not be everywhere at the same time, but with the slim resources available to us, we can make the border a safer place than it would be if we were not present." Levi defended his proposal in a deliberate manner.

The group collectively shook their heads in agreement to Levi's plan. "I can't argue against your proposal, Levi," Phineas smiled. "I was wise in asking you to be second in command. Now, we should return to our homes and prepare. Levi, you and I can get together this winter to settle questions of areas of responsibility, line of communications, and, most of all, our supply line. Each of you should select a suitable mount for the coming operation and see that your families are well cared for by neighbors."

Phineas returned to his home and family. He had four children, and his wife was pregnant again. Their first born were twin boys, Simon and Willard. Their happiness was shattered when Simon died in his sleep a short time after he was born. Therefore, he and his distraught wife named their next son Simon. Three sons and a daughter filled their small cabin to capacity. Phineas increased the acreage he was tilling to feed his growing family. Winters were long and difficult, but they were tolerated with relief, for the threat of Indian attack disappeared when the snow was deep.

Families on the frontier grew a lot of corn because it was easy to grow and to store. It was a nourishing food supply all winter long. Apples, pears and plums were cut into thin slices and strung on flax lines hung above the fireplace to dry. Phineas did not grow any apple trees on his property, but he did raise large quantities of squash and pumpkins which he traded with Levi Wilson for apples from their large apple and peach orchard on a prominent hilltop in New Boston, about forty miles away.

Travel that winter was difficult because the snow was deep and temperatures plummeted below normal in January and February. It was a time when families, isolated from their neighbors, maintained the home fires and spent long hours together slicing apples to dry, spinning flax, making candles by dipping flax wicks repeatedly in melted tallow, and fabricating clothes for the entire family. It was during those long winter days and nights that the family was able to work together as a team, strengthening the family bonds. The sound of laughter often filled the snowbound cabin.

The threat of Indian attack was diminished, but never completely dismissed. The family rehearsed their roles if such an attack did take place. Phineas maintained his firearms in good condition. The flintlock musket and pistols were always loaded and primed, ready for instant use if the need arose. The children were warned to seek the shelter of the root cellar, a large hole dug in the earth beneath the floor of the cabin in front of the fireplace where they stored potatoes, apples, squash and dried fish fillets and venison strips. Phineas was hopeful that if he was killed, the family would survive in case the cabin was set afire. The floor covering the root cellar was made from dense hardwood trees split in half. In time they would burn, but it would take them longer to be ignited than the more flammable pine, hemlock and cedar logs in the walls of the cabin. His hope was that they could survive destruction of the main walls and roof of the cabin. A barrel of water was maintained for the most drastic eventuality.

Phineas dutifully tended his 12 chickens, two horses and the prized Jersey cow that was kept in a barn attached to the north section of the cabin. He was especially proud of the two horses – a young gelding for riding and pulling a small wagon, and a powerful Belgian draft horse that proved to be an invaluable companion on their small family farm.

That winter, Phineas spent a lot of time thinking about the responsibilities he assumed as an officer in the militia. The orders that accompanied his commission specified that he set up routine patrols of the most threatened sections of the frontier. He preferred to remain close to the construction of Fort Number Four and chose to supervise the patrols by working out of the fort about thirty miles east of the small settlement of Hillsboro. The Connecticut River was the favored route for the Abenaki from St. Francis; therefore, he concentrated the bulk of his men scouting both sides of the river. Very few settlers had dared to venture into the area west of the river, but it had to be patrolled so as to keep track of hostile Indian activities.

The area east of Hillsboro became the responsibility of Levi Wilson, an energetic and wily eighteen-year-old volunteer from the small hamlet known as New Boston. His father had two brothers, each with large families, which had emigrated and settled upon a prominent hilltop in the eastern section of the community. The soil was rich and fertile and held moisture for a long time. It was ideal for raising apples and peaches. The families had completely cleared the ridge that ran north-south, and planted fruit trees. After a few years, the trees produced large crops of the staple fruit. Apple pie was frequently available on a daily basis for as long as the apples lasted. When whole apples were no longer available, dried apple slices were reconstituted by soaking them in a pan of water.

The volunteers that were asked to leave their homes were a source of concern to Phineas. The family's loss of the man of the household during planting, cultivating and harvesting time constituted a very real hardship. He encouraged community assistance and asked neighbors to assist the needy families. It was a common occurrence, and it was only fair that each household share some of the burden. The sacrifice of the select few benefited everybody.

Levi Wilson assumed his section of responsibility east of Hillsboro to the Merrimack River, extending about twenty miles east of the river into Fremont. A patrol out of Exeter assumed the stretch eastward to the Piscataqua River. Couriers were to maintain a steady flow of communications back to Number Four so that Lieutenant Phineas Stevens could maintain an overall view of enemy activity within the frontier for which he was primarily responsible.

About mid-April, Levi decided to hold a conference with the men assigned to his patrol. They met at the great falls on the Merrimack River near the new town of Derryfield. The river was teeming with eels, shad, whitefish, and assorted varieties of fish at the rich feeding grounds. The falls was filled with a large number of men, some of them friendly nearby Indians, netting and spearing fish. A small house had been built on the eastern edge of the river by the Stark family. Levi went directly to the house where he met John Stark, a brusque, muscular man about his age. They had met a year earlier when the Stark family moved from Londonderry to the edge of the frontier at Derryfield. Levi and his father had helped them build a shed onto the north end of the house for the storage of firewood.

John Stark was an energetic, stocky man with large bushy eyebrows and deep-set eyes that shined bright and seemed to look through a person. Levi had found them intimidating at first, but he soon found that Stark was quite congenial with a quick mind and an independent streak. He was a man of few words, but when he did speak, people listened. He was soft spoken with a courteous mannerism and was always in control of himself. There was a spring to his step, and he moved about effortlessly. Everywhere he went he rode a fine horse which he mounted and rode with grace in motion.

Levi met Stark in the woodshed. "It's good to see you again, John."

John drove the axe he was using to split wood into the chopping block and turned toward Levi. "I'm glad to see you,

Levi. The winter has been long. I've heard you're mounting a border patrol."

"Yes," Levi motioned to the men with him. "We've volunteered to make a show of force, hoping that we can reduce some of the butchery and violence on the frontier. Why don't you join us, John? You're the best shot in the area."

Stark silently evaluated each man with Levi and seemed satisfied that they were up to the task ahead of them. He then looked at Levi with his intense gaze. "Something has got to be done to control the bloodshed and terror that exists out there. I'll sign up for six months and provide my own horse and musket. Forage, grain and other supplies will have to be supplied by the colony."

"That has already been arranged, John. Let me be the first to welcome you to our small band of border riders. Lieutenant Phineas Stevens signed me on as an ensign, second in command. I'll be your boss covering the Merrimack."

John smiled at him. "I'll obey your orders as long as they make sense. If not, I'll tell you right up front what I don't like about them."

Levi shook his hand. "I can't ask for a better arrangement, John."

Two weeks later, the militia was formally sworn in, and they began active patrols. Levi knew John Stark to be a skilled woodsman who did not bow to authority, so he placed him in charge of the patrol covering the eastern side of the Merrimack River while he concentrated on the western portion.

Levi rode with Hasen Poole, a young man from Weare. They planned to head north about 25 miles to a small collection of settlers' cabins called Warner. At that point they would turn east to the Merrimack and then south along the western shore, completing a semi-circle within some of the most threatened territory in New Hampshire.

They stopped at a small stream for a rest and let their horses stand in the water to soak their hooves. Levi had prepared some pemmican, a staple traveling food for the woodsman, Indian or white man. The large leather pouch contained dried venison, dried apples, corn, and dried berries soaked in molasses and mixed in deer tallow. Levi was fond of the food and offered some to Hasen. Suddenly a breeze blew across their faces, and they smelled smoke!

Levi threw the pemmican in his saddlebag and slung himself into the saddle with ease. He and Hasen turned their mounts out of the stream towards the smoke when a sharp report echoed across the landscape. Someone was in trouble, and Levi pushed his Narragansett rapidly through the forest. They climbed a small knoll, looking down on a log cabin that was burning briskly.

"Prime your weapon, Hasen. We're going in fast," he cried out over his shoulder.

The two riders were halfway down the hill entering the clearing when they spotted three Indians running away from them in the opposite direction. Large amounts of smoke from the burning cabin clouded their vision. Levi always carried two pistols in the front of his saddle, with a firelock under his right leg. He drew one of the pistols, contemplating taking a shot at the fleeing Indians, but decided to save his ammunition. He leaped from the saddle and ran toward the burning building. It was fully enveloped. They were too late to see if anyone was inside.

Levi turned to check out the lean-to beside the cabin. Smoke choked him and obscured his vision, but he could see that two pigs and a jersey cow were dead, killed by tomahawk blows to the head. He almost tripped on a dead Indian body with a tomahawk clasped in his hand. He wrenched the axe free and called out, "Is there anyone here that can hear me? The Indians are gone."

A loud, high-pitched scream came from the lean-to in answer to his call. Levi caught Hasen's attention and warned him to stay alert for the return of the raiders, and climbed over a dead horse into the animal shelter. The source of the scream was a woman bending over a dead white man's inert body. His face had been smashed by an Indian tomahawk. The ground was saturated with blood. Nearby, Levi noted an old scattergun. He picked it up and leaned it against the fence rail.

"I'm Levi Wilson of the New Hampshire militia. Have you been hurt?" he asked in a calm voice, carefully placing his pistol and tomahawk beside the dead man's body. The sight of the man's face made him want to retch, but he stubbornly maintained his composure to help the woman who was terrorized and in a state of shock. She had been pushed to the limits of her sanity, and now she simply retreated into an inner world that sheltered her from the horror of what had taken place at their home in the forest.

"There's nothing you can do for him now, lady. Can you tell me what happened? How many Abenaki were there?" he asked, bending over to pick her up. She simply gave him an indifferent stare, uncertain of what was happening. He thought that it was just as well. She continued to be wracked with convulsive cries that softly began in her heart and erupted in a torrent from her trembling lips. He feared that she was going mad, and that frightened him. Hesitant, gasping sounds accompanied her weeping. He placed her outside of the lean-to beyond the still-burning cabin near the two horses.

"Hasen, get one of our blankets and place it on the ground for the lady to lie on," he requested, wary about being in the open. He placed her on the blanket and grabbed his own bedroll to cover the distraught woman curled up in a tight knot in a fetal position. He shook his head and wondered what he would have done if he had been a witness to the same ghastly deeds. "Watch her, Hasen, I'm going to take a run around the clearing to make sure we're alone."

Levi's first stop was to retrieve his pistol and tomahawk from the animal shelter. Looking for footprints in the soft soil, he came around a pile of firewood and tripped over another Indian warrior waiting for him. Levi knew that his only chance of surviving this encounter was his pistol, which he deliberately cocked as he was falling. Landing on his left shoulder, Levi straightened his right arm holding the pistol and squeezed the trigger.

The Indian had leaped on him just as Levi raised his arm. A look of fear passed over his face a fraction of a second before the loud explosion erupted, driving a lead ball into the enemy's throat, tearing a gaping hole. He was dead before he landed on Levi.

"Levi, are you okay?" Hasen cried, afraid for his companion.

"There was another one skulking around in the back," Levi told him in an unsteady voice. It was the first time he had killed a man, and he felt slightly nauseous. He walked quickly to his horse and with shaking fingers reloaded his pistol.

"Should we pursue the others?" Hasen questioned, noticing Levi's uneasiness.

Levi looked at the woman on the blanket and grimaced. "We're vulnerable here in this clearing, Hasen. Let's take the woman and head to Rumford on the Merrimack. The small band that did this has probably fled the area. We should pick up their trail for a mile or so to confirm their direction; then we can turn towards the river. We may have to spend the night in the forest."

Before leaving the clearing, Levi and Hasen circled around the compound making sure that nobody was hiding. As far as they could tell, the only individuals to survive the raid was the woman and the three Indians they saw escaping. They picked up their trail in a northwestern direction. Levi checked the lean-to for any type of hide or blankets that would help keep the lady warm through a night in the forest. He found a horse blanket. Returning to the woman, Hasen and Levi found her sitting up holding a blanket around her. Her eyes were filled with terror, and she was shaking all over.

"I'm sorry that this has happened to you, lady," Levi kneeled down to comfort her. "I'm Levi Wilson, and my friend is Hasen Poole. We're going to take you away from here. Have you been injured?"

She looked at Levi; the fear he saw in her eyes frightened him. She broke into a screeching cry of pain so intense, she passed out and fell to the ground.

"What are we going to do, Levi?"

21

Chapter Three

Standing in the clearing of the compound, Levi, Hasen, and the woman were vulnerable to new attacks if enemy warriors were in the vicinity. Levi was concerned and firmly announced, "We've got to get out of here now. Lift the lady up to me, Hasen. I'll hold her in front of me. Don't forget to bring the two blankets."

Hasen gently lifted the woman up to Levi so that she was straddling the Narragansett. "I'll cut the trail for us. What about her husband?"

"We'll send someone out to bury them. Right now we've got to worry about the woman and get her to safety as soon as possible."

There was still snow in some of the low-lying areas where heavy, overhead canopies prevented the rays of the sun from reaching the ground. They traveled towards the Merrimack River for several miles at a rapid pace. Levi was having trouble holding the woman in front of him. She was still unconscious and leaned forward so much he almost lost her.

"Hasen," he called in a low voice.

Hasen stopped and looked back.

"Give me one of those blankets so that we can tie her to me. Her body is so limp, it's hard to hold her. I hope that she has not been injured. I see no outward signs. It would be nice if we could find some shelter; the night is fast approaching."

The sun was at the horizon, indicating that they had less than an hour of daylight left. Hasen quickly reigned in his horse and pointed ahead. He leaned over the neck of his horse and rode back to Levi about a hundred feet behind him.

"What is it, Hasen?" Levi whispered nervously. The woman was sitting on top of his holstered pistols. He was desperately trying to lift her off so that he could reach one.

"About a hundred yards east of us, I saw a plume of smoke. Possibly a camp fire," Hasen replied in a whisper, pointing to a thin sliver of blue gray smoke wending through the tree tops.

Levi understood the potential danger and motioned for them to backtrack a short distance to a small knoll heavily populated with large hemlock trees. Hasen dismounted and lifted the woman from Levi's horse and placed her against a tree, still bundled in the two blankets. She removed her arms from under the blanket and looked up at him with searching eyes.

Hasen kneeled beside her and calmly told her, "We've spotted a campfire nearby, Ma'am, so please remain quiet until we check it out." She nodded her head, understanding his urgent request.

Levi had tethered the two horses in the thick stand of hemlock and joined Hasen and the woman. "You two stay here. I'll take my two pistols and see what's ahead of us. Don't be alarmed if I'm not back soon. I may decide to wait for total darkness. You two remain alert and be prepared to move out quickly if necessary. We may simply have to skirt around the camp."

"Okay, Levi. Be careful now," Hasen replied, turning to the woman. "I'm not going to leave you here alone."

Levi touched his friend on his shoulder and silently left the secluded hemlock stand. The shadows were rapidly lengthening, and by the time Levi reached a vantage point where he could observe the campfire, darkness had completely enveloped the forest. Slowly and carefully he made his way closer to the fire, checking the ground where he stepped for any dry branches that might signal his presence. He took one of the pistols in his right hand and focused on the scene before him, allowing his eyes to become accustomed to the limited darkness.

He was not frightened, but he was alert and conscious that he might possibly be walking into a trap. Whoever was at the campfire must not have heard their horses, for they continued to talk in low guttural tones. He leaned against a white birch tree and studied the terrain around him. He could see the campfire clearly. The flickering shadows illuminated enough of the surrounding area, indicating that they had camped in a small ravine. Crawling closer to the light, Levi saw two Indians cooking over the fire. His heart was pounding so loud he was afraid they might hear him. Their packs and French firelocks were a few feet from the fire.

To his amazement, a white boy of four or five years walked up to the fire as if to warm himself. One of the Indians took him by the arm and roughly made him sit down, scolding him in language the boy did not understand. He began to cry. The Indian slapped him beside the face, yet the cries continued even louder. An animated conversation began to take place between the two Indians. Levi did not understand the language, but it was evident to him that the two warriors were having a strong disagreement, most likely about the child, and that placed him at the heart of a very dangerous situation.

Levi was uncertain if there were any more Indians in the camp. It was located in a protected area of trees that had been uprooted, exposing granite bedrock beneath the shallow soil. The downed trees gave Levi excellent cover as he carefully lifted himself above the fallen trunks to better observe the trio at the campfire. His first observation of two Indians seemed to be confirmed. The little boy was wearing a shirt and pants woven from flax much like his own. He picked himself up off the ground and placed a floppy rimmed hat on his head that was too big for him. The boy was most likely being taken to the large Indian encampment on the upper coos of the Connecticut River, a popular meeting place for the Abenaki and other Algonquin-speaking tribes.

A full moon was lifting off the eastern horizon, making it easier for Levi to study the area around the campsite. Kneeling beside the fallen trees, Levi checked his two pistols, making sure that they were both primed with powder. He knew that he had recently replaced his flints and was confident that his firearms would not fail him. There was no doubt in his mind what had to be done. He had to retrieve the boy and bring him to his family if they were still alive.

Suddenly, he heard footsteps walking through the forest towards his location. He kneeled beneath the tree trunk and waited. An Indian stood on the tree trunk and urinated a short distance from his hiding spot. If he could overpower the enemy, then the second one at the fireside would be less of a problem. Replacing his pistols in his belt, Levi drew his sharp hunting knife and reached up to yank the Indian off balance. The Indian let out a loud yell as he fell to the ground. Levi instantly drove his knife into his body with every ounce of strength he possessed. The Indian began to thrash around, and Levi repeated the motion several times until his body remained motionless.

Gasping for breath, Levi leaped to his feet, keeping his eyes on the second Indian at the fireside who had picked up a tomahawk and leaped to the outer dark circle of the fire to see what had happened to his companion. Levi calmly paused to aim his pistol at the approaching Indian and pulled the trigger. The Indian collapsed in mid-step. Levi had placed his bullet square in the man's face.

The little boy screamed and started to run away. Levi intercepted him, grabbing him by the arms. "My name is Levi Wilson, young man. Don't be afraid. I'm going to take you home."

Levi checked the campsite and took two deer pelts and a leather pouch of parched corn. Clasping the little boy's hand, they left the desolate scene and hurried to where Hasen was waiting for them. The boy clutched Levi's strong hand. Twice he stumbled and fell, so Levi lifted him onto his shoulders and asked, "What's your name, son?"

"My name is Daniel Ryan," he replied in a trembling voice. "My dad is also Daniel."

"We've got to leave this area in case someone has heard the shot. Hang on tight." Levi retrieved the pelts and corn pouch, then held on to Daniel's legs, picking a route to the hemlock grove.

Hasen and the woman had heard the shot and were afraid for the worst. He strained his eyes in the direction Levi had left them. He might be in trouble! Hasen saw movement where the moonlight shown between the trees and raised his gun.

"It's me, Levi," came a subdued voice. "I'm coming in."

Hasen breathed a sigh of relief and uncocked his musket. "You sure had me scared. What happened?"

"First things first, Hasen. I've got a captive boy here on my shoulders. His name is Daniel. Should we stay put or try to find another camp for the night away from here?"

"There are no trails for us to follow, Levi. I vote to stay here until dawn. We could take turns keeping watch," Hasen quickly suggested.

Levi lifted Daniel off his shoulders and held him in his arms. "I think you're right. This grove of hemlock will give us some protection against the winds." He saw the woman where Hasen had put her and kneeled beside her. "Lady, this little boy was captured by the Indians. He's confused and scared to death. Would you please take him and share your blankets with him?"

She reached out for the boy. At first he did not want to leave Levi's strong arms. "Come, little man, I won't hurt you." She began to cry and held him close to her.

"His name is Daniel, and he's been a very brave little man. We'll see that he gets home shortly." Levi shook his head, knowing that the prospects of his family being alive were slim.

Daniel began to whimper. "Please don't be afraid, Daniel. You're with friends. My name is Beth Baker."

Levi and Hasen heard her utter her name. Levi patted her on the shoulder. "I'm glad we finally know your name, Mrs. Baker. We're going to stay here for the night. In the morning we'll strike out to the east for the Merrimack River. Hasen and I will take turns standing guard, so try to rest the best you can. Tomorrow could be a long, hard journey. I'll get you some pemmican to eat and a deer pelt to place on the ground to keep you from getting wet."

"You and Mr. Poole have been very kind. I thank you for what you've done. I'll care for Daniel. With a deerskin we'll be comfortable for the night."

Levi instructed Hasen to share the food and went to check on the tethered horses. They had finished off the small ration of oats. He brought them closer to the small campsite, removing a deerskin hunting frock from one of his saddlebags and pulling it over him. "I'll take the first watch, Hasen. I'll wake you in a few hours."

Levi positioned himself, leaning against a large hemlock near the spot where Mrs. Baker and Daniel had settled down for the night. It was still, and the night was beautiful with the moon shedding light through the dark canopies overhead. He thought it strange that he could appreciate the beauty of the wilderness after two brutal encounters that resulted in the death of several human beings. He reflected on their death and felt some remorse, but did not dwell on the subject because he had killed in self-defense. The law of survival is the law of the wilderness.

Well into the evening, Levi heard Hasen snore lightly. He smiled and was glad to have the gentle and steady Hasen for a companion and friend. They had spent much time together hunting, fishing and trapping. They shared a fascination and a respect for the wilderness, even for those native inhabitants who had originally claimed the land as their own. There was something unfair and troubling about that, and even though he fought for the rights of settlers to own the land they had purchased, he had a feeling that if he were an Indian, he would object to the invasion of the settlers, too, but he would never resort to the brutalities that were a trademark of the dreaded Abenaki.

Levi wondered about Mrs. Baker and Daniel Ryan. Their names were not on the rough map and list of settlers that Lieutenant Stevens had given to each of the militia leaders. They were probably newcomers. So far, the Abenaki and their French allies had wiped out two families in his patrol district. He lamented that they had not started their patrol a few days earlier.

Near midnight Levi gently aroused Hasen and climbed into the warm deerskin he vacated. The night passed without incident. They were in luck; the day dawned warm and sunny with the sun rising quickly in the eastern quadrant. Levi had watched the rays gently filter through the thick hemlock canopy and stood up to stretch. He first placed the two pistols back in their holsters on the saddle and brought some pemmican and corn to Mrs. Baker and Daniel.

"Did you rest well, Mrs. Baker?" he asked, passing the pouch to her.

She saw him coming. "Yes, better than I expected," she answered soberly. "Daniel slept soundly through the night. How soon will you be starting out?"

"Just as soon as you and Daniel can be ready. There's a small trickle of water running behind you. It should be enough for you to drink and refresh yourselves. I'm going to take the horses a few feet downstream to wet their hooves and to drink. Hasen and I'll be ready when you are."

"Daniel and I will not take long," she promised, uncovering Daniel to fold the blanket and skin.

The forest travelers rode for several hours into the sun as it gradually turned southward on an approximate track toward Rumford. The closer they came to the Merrimack River, the more likely their chance of intercepting some homesteads. The settlers generally claimed land along the river before they moved westerly or northerly, expanding the density of ownership.

Hasen led the party so that he could readily reconnoiter the surrounding territory, with Levi carrying Daniel and Mrs. Baker following in his tracks. There was a small cluster of cabins north of Rumford, bordering the river. Levi anticipated that it might be a safe location for their companions. Several small streams that drained into the large river had to be forded on their way. These open passages were traditionally a favorite location for an Indian attack, and they approached them cautiously. Levi told Hasen to continue across alone while he remained behind in seclusion until the way was clear for them to pass over.

Levi was familiar with the area, for he had hunted and trapped it often, even up to the large mountains to the north, with his father and uncles. He thought about his passengers. Mrs. Baker had been quiet on the trip. She had told him during one of their rest stops that Daniel had confided to her that his mother and father had been killed and scalped before his eyes. Looking now at Daniel, Levi could see the trauma that was still troubling him. He stared off into space for long periods of time and often wept in silence, remembering the horrific scene. His small, fragile body shook and trembled for long periods of time. That memory would probably be with him to his death.

Hasen signaled for them to cross. Levi explained to Mrs. Baker and Daniel, "It's just a short distance now to a small settlement on the river. Where did you live before you and your husband raised the cabin, Mrs. Baker?"

"We spent some time in Londonderry, then my husband took a job in Starktown cutting logs and firewood. We stayed for a while with the Caleb Page family. I worked as a servant for the family while we saved enough money to purchase the homestead," she told him.

She seemed uneasy talking about her past, yet Levi continued questioning her. "Do you or your husband have family nearby? If so, we'll see that you're safely taken there."

The question completely unnerved her. She struggled to control her emotions and answered in a wavering voice, "Both of our parents died from smallpox. We were both indentured to a family in Londonderry. They released us of our commitment if we wished to take a chance on homesteading... I have no place to go, Mr. Wilson."

"I understand," Levi calmly replied. "If you don't mind, I'll take you to my home in New Boston. My father and his two brothers have built homes on a prominent ridge in the town, and you will be welcome by all of them if that's what you want. There's always work to be done on a farm, and you'll not be an intruder. Otherwise, we may stay on the west bank of the river until we arrive at a suitable place for you and Daniel. It's up to you."

"You have been very kind. I'd like to keep Daniel with me until we find out more about his family. He seems to be comfortable with me. His plight has helped me to stop dwelling on the tragedy that took place at our cabin." Tears erupted from her dark brown eyes.

Feeling helpless to console her, Levi motioned to Hasen, "We'll pick a track west of south from here, and head directly for New Boston. Another night in the wilderness will be too hard on our guests."

"I gotcha, Levi," Hasen replied, quickening the pace.

Several hours later, the shadows grew longer as the forest travelers pushed their mounts across the slow moving river located at the foot of the high ridge where the three Wilson brothers had built their homes and established some of the finest apple orchards in the colony.

Familiar surroundings brought a smile to Levi's lips. He directed the faithful Narragansett out of the water up the bank and proudly announced, "We're a few minutes from a warm fire and a soft bed, Mrs. Baker. Welcome to New Boston." He pointed to a well-worn cart track up a steep incline.

Chapter Four

The agrarian community founded by the Wilson brothers soon became known as Wilson Hill. The three Scotch-Irish immigrant families brought apple seeds and potatoes across the Atlantic with them. They were perceived as hard drinkers and quarrelsome roughnecks who preferred the sword to the plow, but exceptions to the rule were plentiful. The families with roots in Northern Ireland shared strong feelings about family honor; displayed courageous martial prowess; and revered the traditions of independence and self-sufficiency. They were ambitious, industrious, and inventive.

The Wilsons established their tracts side by side at the top of the ridge. The location was perfect for orchards with excellent air drainage and deep moist soil that retained its moisture for a long period of time. The fruits of their labor were obvious in the well-cared-for buildings and extensive rolling landscape of apple orchards and recently tilled fields ready for seeding.

The settling of the area added to the tensions building daily on the frontier between the Abenaki and the hardworking frontiersmen. The brothers supported each other and built their fine two-story homes as a statement that they had arrived to stay permanently. When they first moved to the area, it was on the edge of the frontier, subject to the Indian's vengeance for real or imagined wrongs, the primary motivation for the terror that flowed back and forth across the land.

The evening that Hasen and Levi arrived, Levi had pointed out to Mrs. Baker that his Uncle John had the first house on the left side of the roadway while his Uncle Will occupied the second white dwelling several hundred yards apart. His father, Amos Wilson, owned the third house on the opposite side of the road. Amos was a hardworking man. His extensive orchards and fields of corn, potatoes, squash and flax were the envy of his neighbors. In the winter he busied himself and family making candles which he sold all over the county. He was proud of his agricultural pursuits, but his pride and joy was his stable of fine Narragansett horses. Levi had inherited his passion for the gentle and courageous breed.

Hasen accompanied Levi to their dooryard and announced, "I'm heading out for home, Levi."

Levi reigned in his mount and turned to Hasen, "We should return to our assigned area as soon as possible. Could you ride tomorrow to the construction site of Number Four and report our status to Lieutenant Stevens? If he has a more accurate list of settlers in our area, we should have a copy. Our presence must have some deterrence, but we could be more effective if we knew where the new settlers are located. I'll meet you at the burned Baker cabin two days from now. Is that asking too much of you, Hasen?"

"No, I'll be there," Hasen replied, tipping his hat to Mrs. Baker. "I wish you the very best, Mrs. Baker. Goodbye."

Beth Baker reached out to grasp him on the arm. "You and Mr. Wilson have been most kind; I appreciate what you've done. May God guide you on your journey."

It was too dark for Beth Baker to see, but Hasen blushed at her words. "We thank that same God that we came when we did. Goodbye to you, too, Daniel. You've been a strong little boy. Well, I'll meet you in Warner the day after tomorrow, Levi."

"Thanks, Hasen," Levi answered, dismounting. "I'll take Daniel now, Mrs. Baker."

She passed Daniel to him and slid down the side of the Narragansett, looking at the large white house overlooking the orchards. The house and large barn were connected by a low single-story shed structure. Levi tied the horse to a hitching post and guided them to the front door where he called out, "I'm home, and we have a couple of guests."

They stepped through the vestibule into a large kitchen with a fire crackling in the fireplace. They were met by a tall, middle-aged man with a bushy beard. He spoke with a booming voice filled with excitement. "Come in, Lad, you're a welcome sight." He embraced his son, looking over his shoulder at Mrs. Baker and Daniel, and called out, "Mother, our son has come home safe, and we have company."

Levi picked up Daniel and turned to Mrs. Baker. "Father, this is Mrs. Baker. Her husband was killed by Indians. We got there too late to help him. This little man is called Daniel Ryan. He had been taken prisoner by the Indians."

Amos took a closer look at Mrs. Baker, standing alone, frightened, exhausted and filled with despair. "My dear child, you are most welcome in this home. Come take a seat by the fire. You are safe here." He took Daniel from Levi and held him close to his heart. "Ye remind me of my Levi and his brother Eliphalet when they were little boys."

Levi's mother entered the room and ran into her son's arms. Small of frame with sharply chiseled facial features, Maude Wilson was the epitome of a frontier homemaker. She greeted Beth Baker with a warm embrace, welcoming her to their hearth and home. "You must be starved and exhausted from your horrible ordeal."

"Your son and his companion have been very kind." Beth Baker was having a difficult time holding back the tears rushing for release. She was directed to sit down at the large oak table that dominated the kitchen area.

Levi excused himself so that he could care for the faithful Narragansett. The horse had earned a good ration of oats and all the fresh hay she could eat. He first removed his pistols, then the saddle and turned the horse into a large clean stall. Checking to see that water was available for the horse, Levi brought his weapons into the house, placing them on a rack close to the front door. He saw Mrs. Baker and Daniel being escorted upstairs by his mother. He smiled. His gentle and caring mother and his strong compassionate father would be good for the young grieving widow and unfortunate little Daniel he had brought to their home.

Amos Wilson heard his son enter the house. "Your mother has made a fresh hot tea for ye, Lad, and there is a large piece of apple pie here on the table. Ye must be hungry, too."

"I am, Dad." Pouring hot tea in a mug, he sat down beside his father and took a sip. "My, this tastes good."

"Your mother has taken the two upstairs to calm them down. They took some tea, and your mother will bring them something to eat in their room. Your mother thought it best for her to retire to a quiet place where she can feel safe and be comfortable. Ah, these things happen a lot in this new land. This is not the first time we've seen such tragedy. One wonders if peace will ever prevail. The tenacity of the redman is unflinching, and the future does not bode well, Son. We worry much about you out there in the middle of strife and danger."

Levi tasted a mouthful of apple pie, a staple item in the Wilson household. "Your concern is understandable, Father, but I do it because I believe in what we're doing. It's the only way we can be worthy of the land. If we don't have the will to protect what we believe to be ours after we have paid for it and sweated over its improvement, then everything else becomes meaningless. I have great compassion for the Abenaki who roamed this same land for generations. Truly, it must be big enough for all of us to live in harmony and peace if we so desire."

Amos was proud of the fine young man his younger son had become. "I read in the COASTAL BEACON from Portsmouth an article stating that the frontier from the Kennebec River further north to the Hudson to our west has exploded in a new wave of violence. The Abenaki fight for the same reasons that we fight- the land. In the long run, it must be a political settlement. For now, we must confront the terror with an equivalent defensive effort, but I fear things will get worse before they get better."

Levi's mother came down the stairs and entered the kitchen with an empty pail in her hands. There was an estranged look on her face that concerned Levi. "What's wrong, Mother?"

Maude Wilson turned away from the inquiring glances and stared at the glowing embers of the fireplace. Tears came easy to the gentle Maude Wilson, and she finally broke down and openly wept. "That poor, poor child upstairs, Mrs. Baker, has been through more than you imagined, Son."

"What do you mean, Mother?"

"She just told me that she had been raped by three of the Indians while her husband was alive, looking on. He had broken free of his bonds and was killed trying to protect her. The beasts seem to prey upon the helpless and innocent of our people. If I was a man, I could easily become an Indian hunter

33

and kill everyone I found. Little Daniel Ryan has taken to her and fell asleep as soon as we placed him on the bed."

"Now, now, Lass," Amos comforted his wife, placing his arms around her. "Surely, we have to hold ourselves above the inhuman tactics the enemy uses."

Levi remained silent about the news, remembering how Mrs. Baker had reacted to the debauchery of herself and her husband. It was a wonder that she remained as coherent as she did. This was his first involvement in the aftermath of an attack from the Indians, and it triggered a hatred not unlike what his mother expressed.

That next morning, he rode from the house before full light, intent on retracing the route he and Hasen had taken to the Baker cabin. Every fiber of his being was alert to potential dangers in the surrounding wilderness. Both of his pistols were primed in case they were needed in a hurry. The cabin appeared to be the same as they had left it the day before, but closer examination indicated that the savages had returned to desecrate Mrs. Baker's husband's body. The body was laid flat with arms and legs spread outward. His genitals had been severed and grotesquely forced into the dead man's mouth. The sight made him nauseous. Why would any human being want to do such a thing just to leave a defiant message for those who might return to the cabin? Was it to intimidate or to insult? Levi shook his head, filled with rage and disbelief.

His first thought was that the culprits who carried out this revolting deed might still be nearby. Suddenly, his horse heard something from the direction of the lean-to. Driving his heels into the stomach of the Narragansett, Levi wheeled around to leave the compound the same way he entered it, just as two warriors ran from the cabin with bows at the ready. One arrow hit him a glancing blow on his left shoulder blade and entered his body cavity. He reeled from pain, pulling one of the pistols from its holster, shooting the savage. His companion had missed the mark and was busy drawing another arrow from his quiver when Levi pulled his second pistol and hit him in the upper body, spinning the Indian around before he fell to the ground dead.

Out of the corner of his eye, Levi spotted a third Indian running away behind the lean-to. Levi urged the Narragansett after him, knocking him down with the full force of the horse.

He quickly leaped from the saddle with knife in hand and drove the razor-sharp blade twice into the man's chest. The Indian thrashed and cried out several times and fell silent.

Feeling weak and on the verge of vomiting, Levi slowly climbed back into the saddle and calmly reloaded and primed the pans of his two pistols. He was angry at himself. He had hastily ran into a hornet's nest that nearly killed him. His shoulder burned. He knew that the arrow had to be removed soon. He rode away from the opening and into the protection of the thick forest where he reached behind his back and wrenched the arrow from his body. It made him feel faint, and he almost fell out of the saddle. A few minutes passed before his head cleared. He took a long drink of water from his water jug and turned to watch the clearing for a few minutes.

The wound burned and was bleeding, so he tried to cover it with an extra shirt he carried in one of his saddle bags. Fifteen minutes later, he felt strong enough to return to the opening to bury Mr. Baker's body. Locating a shovel in the lean-to, he dug two shovels full, became disoriented, and fell to the ground unconscious. The Narragansett nuzzled his inert body several times.

When Levi next opened his eyes, he was at home in his own bed. His mother was bent over him with a worried look. He had trouble breathing and felt the tight bandages around his chest.

"We've been worried sick about you, Son."

"How did I get here, Mother?"

"Hasen brought you in last night," she replied, placing a second pillow under his head. "You had lost a lot of blood, and the wound on your shoulder penetrated your lungs. The doctor said that you were lucky to survive. There isn't much the doctor can do for you. Regaining your strength is our first priority, Son, and you must rest and drink plenty of liquids. The doctor did cauterize the wound and covered it with sulfur."

"You know, Mother, I'm starved," he said with a grin.

His mother smiled at his statement. "Those words are music to my ears. Be patient a little longer, my son, and I'll have some hot tea up here for you. There's some stewed venison left over from last night."

He turned in bed after his mother left the room and cried out in pain, "Ahh." The effort left him weak and short of breath.

35

Beth Baker entered the room carrying a tray with a pot of tea. She set it down on the small table beside his bed. "Your mother will be up soon with your food. Would you like me to pour some tea for you?"

"That would be great, thank you," he replied, noticing the dark lines under her eyes and the tightness around her mouth. He felt sorry for her. She seemed to be lost in a sea of strangers. "Are you sure that you do not have any families in the colonies, Mrs. Baker?"

She finished pouring tea, avoiding his searching eyes and replied, "I've told you that my immediate family all died from smallpox."

"What about your husband's family?" he persistently inquired, hoping to find something that would bring a spark of life into her tragic circumstance.

There was a hesitation on her part, and he regretted asking the prying questions. "They have their hands full just getting by, and besides, they did not approve of my marriage to their son. Would you like some maple syrup in your tea?"

Levi remembered how his father relished the sweetener on most of his food. "Sure, it does add to the taste. By the way, how is Daniel doing?"

Levi's mother burst into the room with a flourish. "Beth has helped me a lot. She made this venison stew yesterday. Her energy is boundless. It's nice to have another lady around the house. Little Daniel witnessed a scene no human being should ever have to experience, but he is doing well under the circumstances. He'll need some time and a lot of love. He's visiting your Uncle Eric this morning."

He saw how his mother had taken the unfortunate Mrs. Baker and little Daniel under her care, and for the first time he saw the woman smile shyly. "I'm glad for the two of you."

Levi slept for long hours. When he was awake, he drank a lot of tea and broth. He was getting stronger every day even though his breathing was still labored. On the third day of his recovery he was sitting at the oak table in the kitchen, watching the flames in the fireplace, when Lieutenant Stevens visited him.

"I stopped by to check on your progress, Levi. Your father told me what happened." He accepted a cup of tea and took a

36

seat opposite Levi. The sturdy and competent soldier was worried about something.

"It's nice to see you, Lieutenant."

"I just spoke to John Stark, who assumed responsibility for your territory. He's having trouble getting volunteers. I understand your situation, but I wanted to see if you could be ready to resume some of the patrols in a few days?"

"There's nothing I'd rather do, Lieutenant. Sitting around the house is getting me down. The bleeding has stopped, and I'm able to move about some with less pain. I believe I could start limited patrols with Hasen in a few days. By the way, where is Hasen?"

Lieutenant Stevens confided in him. "I sent him on a special mission to Canada. The Jesuits and Abenaki at Odanak have taken some more captives, and they want to ransom them. This has become a profitable enterprise for them. I sent two escorts with Hasen to bring the hostages back home. The French have guaranteed their safety."

"Can they be trusted?" Levi asked sarcastically.

Lieutenant Stevens shrugged his shoulders, "I have to say yes. Some of the French officers are honorable men. I cannot say the same about the Jesuits. When Hasen and the two escorts have completed their task, I'll send him along to your place."

"I'll be ready even if I have to wrap myself like a mummy."

"Before I leave, I want to share some good news with you, Levi."

"I'll take all the good news you can spare," Levi grinned.

"Well, I have just received a captain's commission in the British army and have been ordered to garrison Fort Number Four at Charlestown. Those same orders instruct me to use half of the force for garrison protection and half for periodic patrols within a reasonable distance from the fort in the New Hampshire Grants area. That would contribute to the security and integrity of the fort itself. My commission came from Governor Shirley of Massachusetts. Governor Benning Wentworth of New Hampshire approves of the appointment and will send supplies and equipment for the garrison."

"I'm glad for you, Captain Stevens. You work hard, and the people will be well served by your interpretation of duty."

"Thanks, Levi. I had another reason for stopping by to see you. When I take over the British army troops, I was hoping that

I could convince you to take over the responsibility for the militia patrols beyond what the British army troops can efficiently handle."

Levi thought about the offer and was pleased to learn that Stevens had that kind of confidence in his abilities. "You realize that I'm only eighteen years old, and older volunteers will have trouble taking orders from a younger, relatively inexperienced man."

"I talked with your father in the barn before I came in to see you. The fact that it takes you away from responsibilities on the farm is of course a factor, but he told me directly that you would be able to handle the men and do a good job."

Levi returned Captain Steven's sheepish grin and replied, "With an endorsement like that, how could I graciously refuse?"

"I forgot to tell you something. The New Hampshire Assembly has agreed to authorize you a lieutenant commission in the New Hampshire Militia if you accept the position."

Chapter Five

Levi rested for the next two days and felt much improved. His lung puncture was healing slowly. He could breathe easier than the day Captain Stevens visited him. During that period, Levi thought about the promotion offered to him and the militia unit he would be responsible for. His father had talked about the time he had served in the British army before coming to the colonies. Evidently light infantry units had been formed as special task forces in need of mobility, speed and endurance for long distance penetration of enemy territory. He had read everything he could get his hands on about military affairs since he was a little boy. His mother and father had taught him and his brother how to read and write. He was comfortable putting his thoughts into words on paper. His mother had once told him that he was a good writer with fair penmanship.

Over the years, Levi and his family had carried on an extensive correspondence with Daniel Cullen, publisher of *COASTAL BEACON*, a newspaper from Portsmouth, New Hampshire. While he was waiting for Hasen to show up, he had written a letter to Mr. Cullen to advertise for volunteers for the very special forest patrol unit he anticipated. One requirement was that they provide their own horse, an animal that was gentle, not gunfire shy, capable of quick bursts of speed, and was of a relative small size similar to that of a Narragansett.

Aside from being in good physical condition, and between the ages of 16 and 35 years old, each volunteer should also be able to load and shoot three shots a minute from a musket. Levi visualized a cadre of well-disciplined men to act as a nucleus for larger units if the need arose. He spent long evenings writing in his journal about the organization and tactics the unit

39

would use in the forest. The first thing he wanted to improve was the firearm and the uniform of each volunteer.

His Uncle Eric had been a soldier longer than Uncle John or his father, and he suggested some modifications to the musket. A short, sturdy carbine capable of handling maximum powder charges with a rifled barrel was a more potent shoulder weapon. Such a firearm was easier to use in the forest or on horseback. The shorter barrel might not be as accurate for long distance as the conventional barrel, but it would outperform the existing long barrel smoothbore musket, the popular "Brown Bess" then in use in the British army. Levi was reassured by his Uncle Eric that a blacksmith and gunsmith in Londonderry was capable of turning out the type of weapons he required and thought it would be smart to begin with the conventional "Brown Bess" and modify it as needed. Levi was pleased to resolve that requirement and thanked his Uncle Eric.

The limited experience Levi had in the forest was sufficient for him to know that colorful clothing such as the red tunics worn by the British was inappropriate for clandestine forest operations. He had found that a doeskin hunting frock was one of the most comfortable and durable garments, and decided that it would be worn by all of the volunteers. Pant wear could be the choice of the man, but it should blend well into the forest scenery. When patrols in the dead of winter were required, the men could use fur garments of choice. Survival in severe winter was paramount and superseded uniformity of clothing.

The day after Captain Stevens left New Boston, Levi and his father traveled to Exeter to discuss things with the New Hampshire Assembly and Governor Benning Wentworth to seek financial assistance for his special forest patrols. They crossed the Merrimack River on the ferry at Derryfield just south of the large falls where John Stark's family had built a home on the east bank. Once across, they rode through Londonderry, arriving at Exeter by mid-afternoon. Amos knew the Governor on a first-name basis, and they were quickly escorted into his office.

Benning Wentworth was a short, portly man with a stern, even an arrogant, demeanor, but he smiled at Amos and shook his hand. He told them that he was glad to hear of their plans for a border ranging patrol in the frontier wilderness. It would provide some element of protection against the French and the

Abenaki who were most active in the upper Coos region of the Connecticut River. The Governor suggested that they liaison with Captain Stevens at Fort Number Four. Levi was enthusiastic about the proposal he had outlined to the Governor, and he in turn, was impressed with Levi's mature judgment and intelligence. Levi was quick to inform Governor Benning that he intended to work closely with Captain Stevens.

"I understand that New Hampshire has offered me a lieutenant commission in the New Hampshire Militia," Levi was hesitant to bring the subject up, but his father urged him to settle the offering at this audience with the Governor.

Benning evaluated the husky young farmer standing uneasily before him and replied, "Captain Stevens was correct about the commission. We have not assigned the responsibility yet. Just today we received a letter by courier from Captain Stevens, and he had many good things to say about you, young man. Your proposals for a small elite unit of fifteen to twenty men to act as scouts and protectors of the border region sounds most interesting to me. There is a definite need for such a force, and the quicker we get it into the field, the more lives we'll save. I'll present your plans to the assembly at the next meeting. In the meantime, I urge you to continue with your plans to recruit, train and equip such a group. Thank you for discussing it with me. You have a son to be proud of here, Amos."

"We thank you, Governor, for all your help."

Levi and his father left the assembly hall and stayed overnight at a nearby tavern. His father told him that he was surprised that the Governor met him with such an affable demeanor, for he had the reputation of being haughty and displaying elitist mannerisms. Levi had been impressed with the Governor's acceptance of such a force.

"Well, Son," Amos continued. "Just maybe the man realized that he should have been the one to organize and field such a unit long before this. Now he'll take credit for your future success, and if by chance you fail, then he can blame you. In a sense you handed him a perfect solution to a problem he's neglected for a long time."

Levi shook his head at his father's irreverent remarks and went to bed conscious of the pressure the trip had imposed on him to succeed. One item he was still thinking about was some form of distinctive headgear that would be compatible with forest travel. It had to be comfortable, lightweight, protective in the rain and sun and be inexpensive to make. The popular round floppy rim hat was just not suitable for horseback or brush travel. Again, his father and uncles came to his rescue. He had seen many painted pictures of British troops, and he remembered one Scottish regiment that wore a simple and neat skullcap called a Glengarry. It is a woolen cap creased lengthwise across the top and named after a valley in Scotland. It was capable of readily shedding water and was most comfortable. That evening at the tavern in Exeter, he decided to make that a part of his regular uniform makeup. He did not want to look like fancy gentlemen in some of the British army regiments. He wanted it to be practical, comfortable, long-wearing, and consistent so that he and his men would be recognized for what they were at a distance and distinguishable from normal militia.

That night he dreamed of leading a small band of dedicated patriots into the wilderness in defense of helpless homesteaders, hoping that their courage and tenacity would act as a deterrent. Their goal of bringing peace and stability to the frontier was a noble cause, and Levi was proud to be a part of that effort.

Levi and his father left Exeter early the next morning buoyed by the prospects that the New Hampshire Assembly would vote favorably for their request. The ride home in the wagon aggravated Levi's lungs and aching body more than if they had ridden horseback. Just as soon as they arrived at home, he had a bowl of oatmeal and went directly to bed.

The next day he awoke from a sound, restful sleep listening to his Uncle Eric talking to his father downstairs in the kitchen, and quickly dressed to join them. When he entered the kitchen they were talking about the speed of loading and firing the British army's standard long land service musket affectionately called "Brown Bess". There were several packets of gunpowder and bullets on the kitchen table.

"Ah, the sleepy head arises," chided his Uncle Eric. "Sit down, Lad. I've got something to show you."

"Good-morning, Uncle. I guess father has told you about our trip to Exeter." Levi poured himself a hot mug of tea from the pot on the fireplace grate and sat opposite his Uncle Eric.

"It looks good for your proposal, Lad. I've come early to talk about paper powder packets. Now, you're familiar with the regulation packets used by the British army - a precise amount of 8 grams of powder in a sealed paper wrapper. The standard procedure is to tear off one end of the packet and pour the powder down the barrel, saving enough to fill the firelock's pan. Then the lead bullet is dropped into the barrel and rammed home with the wooden ramrod, or in extreme circumstances, the butt of the musket is stomped on the ground to seat the bullet and charge of powder."

Levi was an excellent shooter and followed his Uncle's description with interest. "Yes, I've seen that work, Uncle."

"Well, Lad, the blacksmith suggested that the Brown Bess muskets be used as a basic weapon for your border riders along with some modifications to make it more accurate and lighter to use. He came up with an idea that I'm surprised hasn't been thought of before."

"What is that, Uncle?"

Levi's father picked up two of the paper packets on the table and placed them in front of his son. "Here's a sample packet, Son."

Uncle Eric enthusiastically continued to explain. Levi had rarely seen his Uncle so exuberant for he had a reputation of being "distant" and avoided casual chatter. "You'll note that the packet has three segments sealed from each other. The larger charge of powder is torn off by the shooter's teeth, and the smaller charge is retained in his mouth while he dumps the powder followed by the bullet and the rest of the paper packet, which can act as a wad to hold the charge secure within the barrel and is rammed home. The smaller packet of powder is then used to charge the pan. You'll note that the packet has three segments separated from each other. The significance of the packet suggested by my blacksmith friend is that all of the charges are pre-measured and therefore will give consistent results. It also eliminates the need of guessing how much powder to leave in the packet for the pan, and it eliminates the movement needed to place the lead bullet in the muzzle. The paper wad also automatically secures the charge in the barrel."

"I can see where it would give a person a decided edge in an engagement," Levi admitted, closely examining one of the wax or tallow-covered paper packets. "I still would want to have my powder horn with me, however."

43

"Of course, Lad," Uncle Eric agreed. "You would need that as a standby alternative in case you ran out of packets. I've tried this new packet, and a man can fire four rounds a minute compared to two or three rounds a minute using the standard army powder packets. The difference could mean life or death."

"It's a novel idea, Uncle."

"I agree with Levi, Eric," Amos Wilson rose from his chair to fill his bowl with oatmeal. "Do ye want some more, Eric?"

"No thanks, Amos. I'm full and must be about my morning chores at the farm." Uncle Eric gathered up the packets on the table and placed them in his pocket. He turned to Levi and said, "I've taken the liberty of requesting the blacksmith to produce all of the packets he has powder for, anticipating that you will be successful in obtaining a grant from the Assembly. Captain Stevens has already made available to the blacksmith a number of muskets for modification. He's a good man, and we are well served by his dedication as an officer. He thinks highly of you, my nephew, and that you should consider an honor coming from a man of his caliber."

Levi blushed, moved by the compliment, knowing that his Uncle liked straight talk. "Thanks for telling me, Uncle Eric. Captain Stevens has always had my respect. His knowledge of frontier warfare is perhaps greater than any other man. It's a privilege to serve under him."

Amos Wilson smiled at his son. "Ye have made us all proud, Lad; that's for sure. This new venture that you're preparing for is sorely needed on the frontier, and we are all thankful that you've shouldered that responsibility the way that you have." He served his son a hearty helping of oatmeal and walked out the door with his brother to the barn.

"Thanks for your help, Uncle Eric."

Levi heard his mother and Mrs. Baker laughing in the room off the kitchen where they made candles and soap. They were dipping candles in a large cast iron pot of beeswax and tallow with ground up bayberries for a clean fragrance. It had been a long time since he had heard his mother laugh like that. His older brother, Eliphalet Jonathon, had died of smallpox two years before. His death had changed his mother. Mrs. Baker helped her with the multitude of work necessary in maintaining a home and a family. Her presence was a welcome addition, and the family was pleased with her willingness to do her part.

It was not long before they realized that Beth Baker was a very intelligent lady capable of reading and writing. She was an admirer of the small library of books in the Wilson sitting room on the south side of the house. She was fond of poetry, especially the works of Geoffrey Chaucer, Christopher Marlowe and Edmund Spencer. She spent idle hours quietly reading and reflecting on her situation. There was often a sad, faraway look in her eyes that continued to touch the Wilson family. Her determination to not be a nuisance motivated her to greater efforts than Levi's mother felt necessary, and she was often scolded for working too hard.

She and Daniel were very close. He clung to her throughout the day. She responded with compassion and patience for his welfare. He walked into the kitchen rubbing his eyes after a sound sleep and unconsciously placed his back to the warmth from the fire. He was shy and looked apprehensively at Levi.

"Hello, Daniel. We haven't had much time to get acquainted since you became a part of the family. Would you like some oatmeal?" Levi asked.

He eyed what Levi was eating and shook his head, "Yes."

Levi poured some extra maple syrup on the bowl Beth had placed in front of him. The simple act drew a smile from Daniel. "I like the syrup."

Levi finished his breakfast and went into the workshop to see if his mother needed anything. She was dipping candles and did not notice his presence. "Good morning, Mom."

Holding the stick of candles level, Mrs. Wilson saw Levi out of the corner of her eyes. "It's nice to see you up and around, Son. How do you feel after your trip to Exeter?"

"I'm doing better, Mother. A little weak still, but I'm almost ready for another patrol with Hasen. Good morning to you, too, Mrs. Baker," acknowledging her with a smile.

"It is a nice morning, too, Mr. Wilson," she replied shyly.

Mrs. Wilson hung her string of candles between two boards and turned to give Levi a big hug. "You worry your mother, Son. A part of me dies every time I see you leave for the frontier. I pray that someone else will shoulder the burden."

Levi embraced his soft and gentle Mother, holding her in his arms. "We've had this conversation a number of times, Mother. The most important responsibility we have on the frontier is to make it as safe as possible. The future of our new world depends on our success. Someday we'll look back upon these times and be proud of our ability to share the land and to extend the hand of friendship to the original inhabitants of the land. I do not blame the Indians as much as I blame the conniving French and their vicious black robe clerics."

Mrs. Baker shook her head in disagreement. "There was a time when I believed and hoped for the same future, Mr. Wilson, but now I only see the Abenaki as evil savages without conscience or humanity."

Levi was about to answer Mrs. Baker when his mother quickly suggested, "Beth, why don't you and Levi drop the formality and call each other by your first names. You're only a year-and-a-half older than he is."

"I'd like that," Beth was quick to reply.

Levi had a bashful streak and blushed easily. "That makes sense to me, too. So, Beth it is from now on." He looked around the room approving of the large number of newly dipped candles they had produced and smiled at Beth. "You do much better work than I do making candles. Mine always came out lumpy."

Beth grinned at him, "That's because you didn't hold them steady while they were drying."

"However, they worked just as well, Son," his Mother added.

"I stopped in to say 'hi' and to let you know that I'm going out for a while. I've got a lot of things to think about, and I can do that better out in the woods than anywhere else. Please don't worry about me, Mother. I'm going to be all right. I'll see you two later this afternoon."

Levi's father helped him saddle his favorite Narragansett. Both father and son had a natural affinity for the solitude and peace they experienced within the forest. Amos Wilson had done the same thing many times. He understood the reason and the necessity.

"So long, Dad. I'll see you later towards evening."

"Whenever the time is right for you, Son."

Levi rode for several miles east until he came to the foothills of the mountain that looked down on the three farms of the Wilson families. He climbed to the top of the northern peak and dismounted on a pleasant overlook where he could

46

see his home and the surrounding fields in the distance. It was a solitary sanctuary he often retreated to when he wanted to be alone. Taking a seat against a white oak tree, he leaned his head against its trunk and closed his eyes so as to give some order to the thoughts that filled his head. A soft, early summer breeze swept across his face, cooling him, brushing away all of the anxieties that had been making him uncomfortable.

The responsibility being placed on his youthful shoulders was unprecedented, and Levi was having serious doubts if he was up to the task. Threatened families and their homes within his sector of the frontier would be depending upon his ability to protect them, or, at the very least, to escort them out of harm's way. It placed a heavy load on him, requiring leadership skills he had not developed and a wily sense of second-guessing their proclaimed enemy. His lack of experience was his greatest disability. He could only make up for the deficiency by being alert and open to suggestions of others who had greater experience as scouts and frontiersmen such as the his Uncle Eric who had presented the idea to him that morning. The fact that he and others were unwavering in their belief in Levi's ability to carry out his assignments gave him a burst of confidence he desperately needed.

The unusual military venture would be a product of his own style of leadership. He had no traditions or tactics to turn to for a precedence. The methods of deployment would be up to him. Once a tactic didn't work, it could be changed, and he found some confidence and relief in the fact that he would not be too rigid in his application of tactics. Flexibility was as important as mobility. The most important factor of all was to bring to every encounter with the enemy a rapid and deadly array of firepower, a prominent display of spirit and boldness, for an intense and short duration. Only then could he be assured that his men would survive to fight again on terms favorable to them. That principle became his main tenet of engagement. In time it would add to their reputation of allusiveness and formidability in a firefight.

Levi wanted more than a regular militia company which frequently had the reputations of sometimes being not much more than an organized mob. The light-infantry battalions of the British army were the closest thing his uncles and father could recall in their collective experience as soldiers. Levi visualized his unit as being more a constabulary force than a military force because he was essentially policing the frontier, not trying to conqueror it.

Regardless of the type of force he would eventually take into the field, strict discipline, evenly applied, and instant adherence to tactical routines would be basic operating principles. Marksmanship and horsemanship were also to be honed to a fine edge in search of excellence. It was firm in his mind that the success of his unit would not be the numbers of dead Indians tallied in his daily log of events. Instead, success would be measured by the numbers of settlers who had bravely placed themselves in danger to carve out of the forest a small piece of land they could call their own. As their numbers increased, so too did the mutual defense of their families. Levi saw it as his responsibility to provide an element of safety against attack until that level of self-defense could be attained.

He found comfort and satisfaction in the conclusions he was mentally storing in his head. The nobility of the task ahead demanded a commensurate effort on his part, and he prayed for the ability to live up to the high standards applied to his responsibility.

Chapter Six

Amos and Eric Wilson donated five young Narragansett horses to Levi's border force. It was approved by Governor Wentworth and the New Hampshire Assembly several days after Levi and his father went to Exeter. Immediately after the news arrived, the entire Wilson clan became involved in equipping and recruiting the authorized border defense force, with Amos Wilson's farm acting as the center of operations.

Governor Wentworth was especially interested in the pacification of the northern portion of the Connecticut River and the junction of the Ammonoosuc. The Upper Coos region was known far and wide by native bands as a fertile growing region with large flat fields capable of yielding bountiful crops every year. It was a popular meeting ground for various tribes who speared and netted fish to dry in the wide open flood plains developed in a shape that looked like an ox-bow. The Governor was concerned that the French might build a fort on the river and was specific in his instructions to Lieutenant Levi Wilson to carefully explore the region to select a suitable site for a fort to be erected in the future if it became necessary to protect English settlers in the region.

Levi discussed his orders with Captain Stevens, and they both agreed that a small mobile force could act as a greater deterrent than a similar force on foot. In a standup fight against French and Indian companies, which frequently numbered twenty to fifty men, the border rangers could only hope to engage in a fighting withdrawal. Stevens was adamant that the mobile force should never seek confrontation with the enemy under any circumstances. If it was unavoidable, it was better to retreat than to stand and fight. A mounted force had the advantages of speed and mobility. They should always use that

49

edge to advantage, never letting the enemy evaluate the size or potential of the mounted troops if possible. Hit-and-run tactics were more effective than decisive stands where one side or the other was annihilated. The ability to fight again in a place and time of more favorable circumstances should be the guiding principle of the mounted border rangers.

Levi was thankful for the assistance and benefit of the wily old Indian fighter's vast experience. Stevens also suggested that Levi take the time he needed to train and equip his recruits, for it was likely that when they did take to the field, they would be responsible for large sections of the frontier that would occupy them for most of the summer period without relief or replenishment of manpower. Hardy young men, unattached to family responsibilities, were a must. Experienced hunters and trackers with a sound knowledge and appreciation of survival in the wilderness was most important.

Captain Stevens left Levi and his father with these words of praise: "This small, elite mounted force you are about to command is going to be the most effective security unit on the border. It may very well be the only one in the field; therefore, great expectations for your success will be widespread and anticipated. If at any time you are in need of reinforcements, supplies or assistance, you have but to ask, and I'll consider it a privilege to comply. You have my sincere best wishes for a successful campaign, Lieutenant Wilson." The veteran officer shook their hands and climbed into his saddle, turning to them with a wide smile. "As you can see, I've been a long-standing admirer of your Narragansett horses and am proud to have purchased this mare from your Uncle Eric. He was reluctant to part with it, but I was persuasive."

The advice from Captain Stevens was sound, reflecting years of campaigning on the frontier. Levi restricted his recruits to young, unmarried men of experience between the age of 18 and 24. Individuals with intelligence and proven physical strength were given precedence. He most certainly did not want an "Indian killer" in the outfit. The recruits were repeatedly told that they were not an assault military force. Their main purpose was to scout the frontier for signs of terror attacks and to prevent them if possible. They were fully capable of holding their own against a similar size enemy force, yet if at all possible, they were to avoid confrontation. In doing so, they would be perceived by their enemies, either Indian or French, as an elusive force of unknown capabilities, thus increasing their deterrent value over and above their diminutive size. If, in every encounter with an enemy force, the enemy was unable to "take their measure," their stature grew commensurate with their ability to deceive the enemy.

The Wilson families were able to procure a supply of new carbine flintlocks with rifled barrels of a smaller caliber than the traditional English army musket. Each rider would carry one in a scabbard beneath his right leg. The mounted border ranger was well equipped to defend himself and any wary settlers in need of his protection. Besides the rifled carbine, each mount had two pistols in holsters on each side of the saddle readily available for the rider to use. He also carried a tomahawk and a bullet pouch on his waist belt, with a twelve inch knife inserted in his right boot.

Levi selected a portion of the loft in his father's barn for the storage of supplies that were steadily pouring into the Wilson brothers' compound. He took responsibility for the company seriously and made an earnest effort to maintain accurate and up-to-date records of everything purchased and donated to the force. From the earliest genesis of the force he was about to lead, Levi was searching for an appropriate name and solicited opinions from everybody he met. In the end, he simply called it the New Hampshire Border Company and reported it to the Governor and the New Hampshire Assembly in Exeter, letting them know that he was prepared to take them into the field shortly.

The men were as ready as they would ever be, and they yearned for practical field experience operating as a unified command. The company carried eight men on the muster roll, and Levi was certain that every man was capable of taking command if necessary. Fully loaded with supplies for an indefinite stay in the frontier wilderness, they were given two days notice before the date of departure.

The day before they were to leave, Levi was in the kitchen writing a report to Captain Stevens and the Governor about his intentions. Little Daniel was quietly watching him. Without warning, a loud high pitched scream came from Beth's room upstairs. Believing that something horrible had happened, Levi placed his pen on the table and listened to the loud voice of his mother begging Beth to calm down. Suddenly, Beth jumped down the stairway and burst out the front door with screams of excruciating pain and despair. She ran blindly across the yard into the large maple grove east of the house.

It all happened so quickly. Levi's mother rushed into the kitchen. He cried out to her, "What's wrong, Mother? Has Beth injured herself?"

"No... no... it's more than that. I fear for her life! She could hurt herself..."

"Mother!" he screamed, looking into her eyes for some indication of what triggered such a violent response from the young lady. "Listen to me. What happened?"

"I simply told her what the doctor told me. She's pregnant, and she believes it's from the Indians!"

"My God," was all Levi could say before he leaped through the door in pursuit of Beth. His heart pounded, and he prayed that she would not try anything foolish.

Levi ran as fast as his legs could carry him, recalling that lately, Beth had been more withdrawn and reticent than usual. He had been so wrapped up in his own project that he paid little attention to her or to Daniel. His mother had Dr. McCrea from Goffstown look at her. Levi remembered seeing him at the house and had waved to him. He was a frequent visitor when he was in the area. Dr. McCrea had a fondness for the apple pies Mrs. Wilson always had on hand.

A well-worn path ran down to the lip of a ravine that ran north-south along the top of the hill where the three Wilson brothers had built their homes and cleared large sections of land for field and orchard. Their maple sugar orchard was located in the hollow below the rim. Levi desperately called for Beth, receiving no response. Listening carefully for any sound, Levi heard Beth gasp for breath near where he had often stood on a large rock waiting patiently for a deer or moose to appear. It was located near the wet area of the lowland. He ran anxiously to the rock and saw Beth lying on the ground beside it.

"Beth, it's me, Levi."

She gave no sign that he was at her side. Laying his hands on her shoulder to comfort her, she wrenched herself free of his touch. The ground was damp and cool, and the sun was fast settling into the west below the hilltop. He ignored her resistance and tried to lift her off the ground. She resisted his efforts, but she did sit up against the large beech tree that hung over the rock. She cradled her face in her arms and began to cry with long high-pitched howls of despair. Levi removed the light deerskin hunting shirt he was wearing and placed it around Beth's shoulders, all the time trying to console her.

"My mother told me about the news from Dr. McCrea; maybe he's wrong in his diagnosis."

She refused to answer him and wept softly into her arms. Eventually, her body twitches became less frequent. He stayed with her until it became dark, and a damp chill settled into the lowland. He shivered, and he knew that she was cold, also.

"Beth, you're scaring me, and I don't know what to do. I can't, and I won't let you hurt yourself. No matter how long you want to stay here, I'll stay too. Please let me help you back to the house. Mother is worried for your welfare, and so am I. Please, speak to me."

She responded to his pleas in a soft voice he could hardly hear. "It would have been better for me if the savages had killed me instead of impregnating me." She again started to scream.

"You're frightening me with that kind of crazy talk, Beth. The death they had in mind for you would have been so much more hurtful than your situation now. I can never know how you really feel, but those who care for you are willing to help you through this difficult period, and I speak for the entire family." His words calmed her screams, as he firmly held her in his arms.

She replied between labored gasps for breath, "No, you can never know how violated I feel…"

Her body continued to shiver. Her bare arms were cold and clammy. He discovered that she was holding a sharp rock in her right hand, and forcefully removed it, dropping it on the ground.

"No, Beth. What did you hope to accomplish with that rock? Tell me…" he cried. She remained silent.

His imagination began to go to work and fear that she had already done something with the rock empowered him to act. He swept her off the ground and held her in his arms like a small child. How he wished that his mother was there to help him console the distraught Beth. She placed her head against his chest and continued crying.

He started up the hill toward the house, feeling her tense body relax. "Listen to me, Beth. When Hasen and I found you, you were the bravest and most courageous person I've ever known, and I've seen nothing about you during all of the days that you've graced our home that would dispel that impression. I also speak for my mother and father. You've got to draw on that reservoir of strength to help carry you through this difficult period. Will you promise me that you won't do anything to harm yourself or that baby you may be carrying?"

She ever so lightly shook her head in the affirmative. Encouraged by her reply, he quickly carried her up the incline to the inviting warmth of the fireplace, hollering for his parents as he approached the kitchen door. By then, he was exhausted and was afraid he might drop her. Amos Wilson gently took Beth from Levi and placed her on the bench beside the crackling fire.

Levi's mother saw the distraught anguish in her eyes and sat beside her, tears of relief running down her cheeks. "My dear girl, you've given us all a fright, and I'm thankful that my worst fears were not realized. Amos, would you please pour Beth a cup of tea? The girl is chilled to her bones." She left the kitchen and shortly returned with a warm blanket which she wrapped around Beth.

Maude Wilson knew that Beth liked the curd they made almost every day from milk. She had just finished warming a large pan and turned off the liquid whey. The remaining curd was a staple food for the Wilson family, enjoyed by all. Amos especially liked a little bit of salt on his curd. She ladled a portion of curd into a bowl and selected a fresh slice of bread they had just finished baking that afternoon. She placed the bowl on a small table next to the bench and rearranged the blanket around Beth's shoulders.

"A little bit of food along with the hot tea will settle your stomach, my dear girl." Maude embraced Beth and whispered in her ear, "You've been a wonderful addition to our family, Beth, and I want you to know that our home is your home. Do not despair for the child you carry next to your heart, for it is you and you alone who will give it a heart, a brain, and a personality in your image. Don't forget that fact, my dear. God wanted you to be the child's mother because He knew that you had the courage to give it birth, otherwise He would not have selected you."

Levi was never more proud of his Mother than he was during that moment of crisis. Daniel had also been a silent witness to the scene and sensed Beth's despair. He climbed onto the bench and laid his head against her, looking into her swollen eyes.

Levi lit two candles and retreated to the large living room off the kitchen where he completed his letters to Captain Stevens and Governor Wentworth. Still troubled with doubts about his ability to head such an endeavor, he voiced those feelings to his father recently and was comforted by his words.

"My young Son," his father had begun, placing his arm over Levi's shoulder. "If yea did not have such doubts, I'd be concerned, too. It's important that we approach every responsibility placed upon our shoulders with all the energy and skill we can bring to bear. Recognizing our limitations is only natural, and perhaps what other people of authority think of our ability is more important than what we think of ourselves. Trust the values others have seen in you, Lad. Authority is a humbling experience, and all great leaders are amply endowed with that virtue."

Tomorrow would prove to be a very busy day for him and the eight men selected to be a part of the operation. He was proud, excited, and worried all at the same time, wondering if there was something he had neglected to consider that might contribute to a successful first patrol. Western civilization was colliding with an ancient way of life that had served the native people for centuries. That fact guaranteed a long, vicious struggle.

That night, after his family and Beth had settled down, Levi crawled into his bed, physically and emotionally exhausted. He no sooner laid his head against the pillow than he heard the calls of the whippoorwills beyond his window. It was a soothing call that never failed to please him. He had never seen the birds in daylight and was unable to locate their exact position at nighttime. The sounds always came at about the same time in the evening and lulled him to sleep. It was a treasured memory of his childhood, and, that evening, he reflected, may have been the last day of his carefree childhood period. In the morning, he would shoulder the responsibilities of a man. It was a poignant moment that he never forgot.

Chapter Seven

Dawn always came too soon. The sun rose above the twin mountains due east of the house and sent rays into his room across the bed. Levi rubbed his eyes and quickly dressed. He could hardly contain the pounding of his heart as he raced down the stairway to the welcome warmth of the fireplace. His mother and Beth were sitting at the table eating oatmeal. He studied Beth, noting the dark circles and the deep lines under her eyes.

His mother turned to look at him and pointed to the large pan on the fireplace grill. "There's plenty of oatmeal for you, Son. If I had the power to keep you here safe on the farm, I'd do it. But, your father did the same thing when he was your age by going off and joining the army." She shrugged her shoulders and plucked a stray thread of hair from her face.

"Someday the frontier will be pacified, Mother," he replied absently. "How are you doing, Beth?"

She was reluctant to meet his searching eyes, for she knew how distraught she must look. "Your mother and father have been kind to offer me a chance to stay with them. For that and for your very kind words I'm thankful and appreciative, but I may never forgive the God who allowed me to conceive a child during such a brutal and violent act of lust." Tears formed in the corner of her eyes. She quickly brushed them away and continued to eat her oatmeal.

Levi ate in silence. What could he say to make her feel better? Her description of the act was accurate. Who was he to minimize the situation? He wondered how he would react if he was in her place? He sympathized for her predicament and was thankful that his mother was there to help her through the challenging times ahead.

Twenty minutes later, he embraced his mother, squeezed Beth's hands, and headed for the barn where his father was waiting for him with his favorite Narragansett, ready and saddled. Two storage sacks filled to capacity with food were attached to the saddle on each side. Two blankets and two tanned deer hides were snugly rolled up and tied to the rear of his saddle. He smiled; his father had thought of everything.

"I've primed and loaded your two pistols and the carbine. I sure do like the way that carbine comes to the shoulder. You have one of the best shoulder weapons on the frontier, Son. I hope you never have to use it," his father told him.

The two embraced each other. Levi felt the tenseness in his father's strong arms. His father hid his emotions most of the time, but, that morning, he saw a moist film cloud his father's vision.

"Thanks for everything, Father. By the way, tell little Daniel that I'll see him when I return, and maybe we could go fishing together. I'll be careful and won't take any unnecessary chances," Levi promised. "My only doubt is that I won't measure up to the responsibility. I'm thankful that most of the men have experience hunting, trapping, and fishing in the wilderness. We're assembling at Rumford on the Merrimack. Hasen will meet us there. Angus Campbell agreed to meet me at the foot of the hill at the river and will accompany me to the rendezvous. He's a great source of strength to me."

Amos stood back to let his son climb into the saddle. "His father and I have been good friends for years. The boards for our house were sawed on his sawmill." Amos guided the horse out of the barn where he held the reigns and looked into his son's eyes. "Don't forget, Son. Keep the couriers busy delivering any information you may gather, even if the patrols are uneventful. The intelligence you send is important to Captain Stevens and the rest of us. May God guide your footsteps. Watch your backside, Son."

Beth and his mother were standing in the barn door opening. He saw the forlorn look on both of their faces. He quickly dismounted and swept his mother in his arms. How he loved her gentle, caring ways! He turned to say good-bye to Beth. "You take good care of my mother and father for me, Beth. I wish you well in every way."

He offered his hand to her. She brushed it aside and kissed him on the cheek. "You be careful, Levi Wilson. You'll be in our prayers, always. Thank you for caring."

Levi blushed self-consciously and climbed into the saddle. He nudged the Narragansett to a canter and headed down the hill with a lump in his throat. Angus was waiting for him on the bank of the river. The two rode side by side and plunged into the water on a northern track.

Two hours later, they met the men at their designated spot on the Merrimack River where a small creek entered the large stream. Hasen saw them first and waved. Levi noted the seven men standing around a small fire. The green caps and the brown hunting frocks distinguished them from most forest travelers. A feeling of pride flowed over him. Even at a distance, their sturdy physiques and confident air presented a formidable appearance of strength and authority. What a privilege it was to be selected as a leader of such hardy frontiersmen.

Raids throughout the frontier were increasing with Fort Number Four at the heart of the struggle. The Abenaki villages on the northern shore of Lake Champlain, Missisquoi; the encampment at Odanak on the St. Lawrence and St. Francis Rivers; and the smaller village further north on the St. Lawrence River at Becancour permanently housed the active participants within the greater New Hampshire frontier. Captain Stevens had informed Levi that between six and seven hundred Abenakis and Penacook Indians inhabited the region between Lake Memphramagog and the Umbagog region in Northern New England and southern Canada. Approximately three hundred warriors could be mustered from that source.

Levi had heard of a white man who had been captured by the Abenaki in 1707 and was adopted as a native son. Later, he returned to the white community and organized a special force to defend the settlers from Indian forays on the frontier which was then much closer to the greater Boston area. His group of bordermen were called "Black Boys." The purpose of organizing a militia type force to defend rights and property of citizens from their enemies was not a new concept. It was a natural manifestation of self-preservation.

Everyone on the frontier realized that the French and Indians were not the only source of trouble. Thieves, smugglers, traders, and trappers also contributed to the turbulent atmosphere. Some homesteaders purchased their lands and honestly believed it was theirs to use as they pleased. Others squatted on Indian lands, depriving the native population of their traditional and natural hunting grounds and cornfields. This forced many of the natives to steal supplies to survive.

At any single time, a hundred different bands of four to twenty Indians could be roaming the northern frontier looking for "targets of opportunity." The Border Company could never counter that many adversaries, but they did hope to be able to track and report on the activities of a percentage of the enemy agents in the field. Knowledge of potential threats and the consequent warning of those targeted by the threat was a valuable tool that heretofore had not been available to the isolated settlers and their families.

Levi, with Captain Stevens's assistance, helped to formulate a plan of action for the company. The initial eight men would take to the field in two-men units. The area they had to cover was immense, and Stevens was enthusiastic about the use of horses for the patrols. They were capable of covering more distance in a day than a man on foot burdened down with necessary supplies to survive an extended stay in the northern wilderness. The native population was skilled in reading forest signs, and both Captain Stevens and Levi believed that tracks had the potential of working in their favor, provided they paid strict attention to their back trail at all times. If the enemy knew that several mounted patrols were in the vicinity, it could help to dampen their zeal. Over a period of time, the company might take on an elusive significance in the mystical realm in which the Indians functioned. In time, it was hoped by all that the company could create a restraint on enemy activities in a far greater proportion than their small numbers would indicate.

There was an inherent anxiety about their effectiveness, harbored by each of the men, and they readily discussed their feelings at the meeting. The company was to stay a month within their assigned areas before being rotated back home for rest and refurbishment. They would be replaced by another party of volunteers being raised at the Wilson farm in New Boston. This long-term deployment implied that the two-men crews would have to live off the land to the best of their ability.

The crews and areas of responsibility were assigned by Levi. He stayed with Angus Campbell of New Boston and John Thompson of Goffstown and took on the largest and most active area on the frontier, the rolling hill section east of the Connecticut River west to the Sunapee Lake region and to the north as far as the junction of the Connecticut and Ammonoosuc Rivers, a section of the fertile valley known locally as the "Upper Cowase."

Allen Warren of Deerfield and Mike O'Malley took the region east of the Sunapee to the Merrimack River. Hasen Poole from Weare and Tom Sullivan of Portsmouth accepted the area west of the Merrimack River to Wolfeboro on the east side of Lake Winnipesaukee. The most easterly region from Wolfeboro to both sides of the Piscataqua River was assigned to Merle Perkins of York and Earl Berry of Exeter. Levi advised all of them to cover the lower foothills of the great mountain chain to the north in a zigzag fashion, covering the full breadth of their respective regions. Once they had arrived at the foothills, they were to reverse course and head south unless they ran into something important, and he left that discretion to each of the men.

An hour or so after they first met, they prepared to take their assigned positions. Levi shook hands with each of them and mounted his Narragansett. He turned to face the company with a serious air. "Remember, you have to take care of yourselves on these patrols. Do not be overzealous to close with the enemy or to take unnecessary chances. Trust your compass to guide you. Your highest priority is to protect lives. The protection of their property is important, but it can be replaced; humans can't. If, in carrying out this order, you have to escort people south to safety, then you must do so together. Maintain your daily journals, noting anything you deem appropriate.

"Avoid a fight if possible. If it cannot be avoided, disengage as soon as the situation dictates. Your survival is more important than anything else. If you kill an enemy, do not take scalps. That is a tactic of savages, and we pride ourselves to be Christians. Reassure the settlers within your sphere of influence and let them know what you are doing. Try to stay with them overnight when feasible. After all, they're the reason for our existence. Any questions?"

61

"If we flush a party of Indians, how far should we go to follow them?" Hasen asked, climbing on his horse.

"That'll be your judgment call, Hasen. Don't be lured into a trap. In general, follow their tracks to determine, to your satisfaction, that they have not spotted you and try to double back to hit you on the flank or the rear. Godspeed to each of you." Levi waved to them and headed west toward the Connecticut River.

Levi, Angus, and John rode westerly to the small cluster of cabins at Walpole on the Connecticut River. From there they turned north following the cart tracks to Fort Number Four at Charlestown, a small community of cabins and homes nestled near the river. The fort was fully manned by British soldiers who hailed them from the elevated lookout station at the southwestern corner of the fort.

Captain Stevens met them as they rode through the main gate, "I expected your visit today or tomorrow, Levi. You've selected some fine horses, and you, Levi, have one of your father's Narragansetts, a good choice."

Levi smiled and dismounted, "How could I do otherwise, Captain? We're weary and hungry from the long ride, and the security of this stockade is welcome."

"Well, we're glad to have you. The guards will take your mounts and care for them. There's hot tea and venison stew in the great room above the entrance. You're welcome to eat your fill and to stay the night. The room is a little crowded now that we have our full complement of soldiers, but there's room for all. I look forward to seeing you often now that you've started your patrols. I don't have to tell you that Indian forays are increasing daily. The frontier around the fort has exploded with violence. I see no end in sight, nor do I see any increase in British soldiers to offset the French and Indian threat to our safety."

The three Border Company members saw the anxious look on the Captain's face. He was in a position to know better than anyone else the situation on the frontier. If he was worried, then things had to be getting out of control. It gave each of them pause about the difference their small detachment of eight men could have in the limitless wilderness that surrounded them. Captain Stevens led them upstairs to the great room above the entrance gate. It was dark except for the large fireplace in the center of the room.

"Make yourselves comfortable, men." Captain Stevens saluted them as an orderly called him from the stairs leading to the lookout platform.

"Thanks, Captain Stevens," Levi replied. "My, that stew smells tempting."

They helped themselves from the large kettle of stew and a boiling pail of strong tea, and sat down near the fireplace to eat. Levi leaned against the wall watching Angus, who was naturally curious about most everything, studying a British soldier's musket.

Angus was a small-framed, wiry young man a year younger than Levi with long blond hair tied in a bunch at the back of his head. The British soldiers impressed him with their military air and the confident way they carried their weapons. Angus was capable of hitting an eight inch target three hundred yards away two out of three times in a minute. He was the best marksman in the company. The soldier also eyed the carbines they were carrying and told Angus that the Long Land Service musket had a 46 inch barrel, used a 1.12 ounce lead bullet with .28 ounce of powder.

Angus proudly told him, "Our carbines were converted from the same musket with a rifled barrel installed. It fires a 1.0 ounce elongated bullet with .40 ounce of powder. It kicks pretty hard, but it can reach out further than your musket, and its faster moving bullet is more deadly to an opponent."

Levi listened to the exchange with interest and told Angus, "You'd better sleep with your carbine at your side, or someone will steal it from you."

They ate in silence for several minutes. Angus watched the flickering light from the fire and turned to Levi. "Do you know, Levi, I'm homesick already. I've been away from home a lot, but my father was always with me. I worked a month on a fishing boat in Portsmouth last summer, but my brother was with me. I didn't think it would bother me, but there it is."

Levi placed his arm around his best friend, "I have to confess that I had the same longings on my first trip with the militia, Angus. Don't worry; it soon goes away. I have something to confess to you and John here. Every time I leave the safety and security of the farm, I'm scared. I know it sounds unheroic, but it's true. My father told me that a man needs a certain amount of fear in order to stay alert. It gives a man the

63

courage to continue with the mission. I suspect that everyone has the same feelings but would not admit it."

Angus and Levi had gone to school together at New Boston and been good friends since they were infants. Angus smiled and looked up to Levi, who was ten inches taller, and said, "I never would have known it. You've always seemed to be in control of yourself, Levi. I'm proud of the way you've taken responsibility for the company; I'm not ready for that yet."

"All you need is a little more experience, Angus, and you'll do just fine. I feel better having you with us. No one can shoot as accurately or as fast as you. So, in a fight you stick close to me," Levi grinned.

They finished eating and relaxed over a second cup of hot tea. John volunteered to check on the horses. He was a slender, lanky young man with long arms and legs — a taciturn individual who rarely shared his thoughts with anyone. He was extremely loyal to Levi in spite of the fact that Levi was four years younger. John returned with all six of their pistols in a leather sack. "There was some unsavory character down there at the stables, so I brought the pistols with me."

"That's a good idea, John," Levi accepted the sack and placed it on his blanket.

"I'm tired, and a good night's sleep will feel good," John casually remarked with a grin. "The first one to snore gets a boot in the rear."

The three slept close to each other in the dark hall. The fire was maintained throughout the night to keep the tea hot. Soldiers stopped by periodically to pour a cup and take it on their watch. As the morning hours approached, the mess attendants piled more wood on the fire and set a large kettle of water on the grates to boil for oatmeal. The men woke to the aroma of food and ate hasty pudding and oatmeal for breakfast.

Levi led the way to the stables on the east side of the fort opposite the Connecticut River. They checked the cinch straps and placed their pistols in the appropriate holsters after priming them with fresh powder. Suddenly shots were heard on the opposite side of the stockade. Return fire erupted from the damp morning air. Levi ordered them to bring the horses inside the stockade. By the time they got there, the shooting continued amidst much shouting and hollering from the river.

Captain Stevens ran past them to check on a soldier who had been wounded. The stockade walls were made by planting ten inch trees and larger in the ground placed four inches apart so that the fence could not be readily burned. The walls were fire resistant but bullets could easily penetrate through the open spaces. Captain Stevens kneeled beside the wounded soldier, and Levi rushed to help him. None of the enemy were visible that he could see. The soldier took a direct hit on his right arm. It was bleeding profusely.

"Are you hit anywhere else, Jenkins?" Captain Stevens calmly asked.

"No, Sir, but they got me good in the arm."

Captain Stevens nodded to Levi, "Can you help me carry him to Dr. Hastings' quarters?"

"Of course," Levi answered, grabbing the soldier's legs. They rushed to the southwest corner of the fort and placed the wounded man on a table for Dr. Hastings to examine him. The Doctor motioned them out the door.

Captain Stevens and Levi returned to the center of the compound where the Captain ordered every available man to the stockade walls and to be alert for a potential attack against the fort, advising them to fire only on specific targets to save ammunition. Then, he grabbed Levi's arm and directed him to the elevated observation platform above the doctor's quarters. They ran up the stairs where two of the soldiers had just fired at a target at the edge of the great meadow next to the bank of the river. Captain Stevens used his telescope to scan the full breadth of the view from the vantage point.

He excitedly passed the scope to Levi and pointed to a location near the settlement of Charlestown south of the fort. "I plainly saw a blue and white French uniform by the river close to the village. Perhaps the shots fired at the fort were a ruse to divert our attention from that area. What do you see, Levi? My eyesight is not very good for long distances."

Levi held the scope steady, focusing on activity at the river's edge. "There's a collection of Indians and French soldiers there. It looks as if they're trying to load supplies into several canoes or boats. I can't see below the vegetation on the bank of the river. Several white people are there. I specifically saw a white woman being led to the water's edge by an Abenaki." Alarmed at what was taking place, Levi was surprised at how

65

calm he was. He handed the scope back to Captain Stevens. "If they have taken hostages, then they probably plan to cross the river to the west side and portage around the fort out of sight and danger."

Captain Stevens observed the scene again. The firing at the fort was sporadic with few Indians presenting themselves. "You're right, Levi. I saw two white women sitting side by side, probably in a canoe."

"What can we do?" Levi asked, his adrenalin beginning to run high.

The commanding officer of the fort gritted his teeth and replied, "We do not have enough men to send out a relief party, and there are no canoes or boats available to cross the river." He handed the scope to one of the soldiers at the lookout and rushed down the stairs to the great chamber filled with anxious civilians and small children. Continuing down the stairs to the stockade compound, they met Angus and John waiting beside their horses.

"Captain," Levi began, thinking about a possible plan. "What do you think about the three of us exiting the stockade on the east side, making a run north beyond sight of anyone at the river's edge to a point where we can cross over the river and backtrack to intercept the party of hostage takers? We might have a chance to catch them off guard while they're still afoot in the forest."

Captain Stevens was hesitant to authorize such a risky enterprise. If he had a troop of cavalry, that would be different, but three men on horseback were outnumbered and could prove to be a disaster. He saw that the three border riders were waiting for his command. They were better armed than the soldiers. He saw no other way and reluctantly gave his permission. "I'll authorize you to pursue the raiders and to interfere with their plans only, I repeat, only, if you have a crystal clear chance for success. Otherwise, you'll succeed in getting the hostages murdered and yourselves killed or wounded. Remember, the hostages have a chance of being ransomed at some later time. Do you understand?"

Levi leaned down to shake Captain Steven's hand, "We won't let you down, Captain." They left the fort at a gallop.

Chapter Eight

Late October, 1781 at Fort Niagara

The wind blowing off Lake Ontario was bone-chilling, a harbinger of deep snows, plunging temperatures, and long winter nights when the wind howled across the frozen lakes and open landscape. Levi Wilson breathed deeply of the cool air, unaffected by its sting. His heart and his soul were transported to the days of yore when he was a young man and had been given a militia commission by the Governor to command the newly formed New Hampshire Border Company. He remembered how it had been in that time of unprecedented terror on the frontier. He also remembered the men who had served their cause so well and were now gone, passed over in the pages of history as if they had never existed, but they were remembered by their leader with a warm glow in his heart.

Long gray hair fell over his ears and down the back of his neck where once it had been black as coal. The courageous soldier was showing his age. A veil of sadness filled his heart. He paid a silent tribute to those who had fallen in the cause of liberty. He held their memory close to his heart and agonized that one hundred years from now, no one will ever know or appreciate just how difficult the struggle for victory had been. They had placed their fragile bodies between the enemy and their loved ones and had gone unheralded. But their spirit, forever young, will be watching down through the ages with sad eyes, remembering what might have been.

Three men instantly came to Levi's recollection — the intrepid Captain Phineas Stevens, a brave and humble soldier; Angus Campbell, a big man in a small body who had saved

Levi's life several times over the turbulent years; and the third man, John Thompson, unflappable, with nerves of steel who followed Levi with unprecedented loyalty and courage. Levi never forgot their baptism of fire at Fort Number Four, the summer of 1745.

* * *

Levi had led John and Angus out of the stockade at a gallop and turned north along the east bank of the Connecticut River for a mile or more until they came to a suitable shallow fording location where the horses would not have to swim. They had checked the loads and priming pans of their weapons before leaving the fort. Nervously watching both banks of the river, Levi was the first to climb onto the western bank into the cover of hemlock and alder trees.

He signaled for John and Angus to come abreast of him. "We should spread out to cover a wide path down the river. The Indians probably won't try to reenter the river until they're well clear of any view from the fort. I'm not sure what we should do, but be on the lookout for a suitable observation site with a little elevation so that we can lie in wait until they come into view."

John and Angus understood. Positioning themselves about fifty yards apart, they began a slow advance down along the river bank, studying the terrain around them. They came to a rock ledge that rose above the surrounding ground about fifteen feet. It was perfect for them to view the bank of the river from a concealed position. They tethered the horses in a thick alder stand next to the ledge, then grabbed their three weapons. Levi was the first to crawl to the lip of the rock outcrop to view the circular basin below. He directed John and Angus on either side of him. The first thing they did was check the priming and flints of their weapons.

Now they were certain that they would be able to intercept the raiding party as it passed their positions. It was a larger band of warriors than they would be able to confront in a pitched engagement, but he whispered that they only need to slow their advance and confront the soldiers and Indians that were keeping guard over the captives. A thin veil of ferns shielded their observation posts from searching eyes. Angus was the first to spot something moving in the distance. Each of them had their weapons ready for instant action.

The first to appear were two Abenaki Indians armed with French muskets. They were alert and scanned the area, looking for the slightest sign of something out of place. Their sharp eyes studied the ledge above them knowing full well that it was a perfect spot for an ambush. Levi anxiously watched the warriors from behind a clump of ferns that concealed his identity. He held his breath as beads of sweat formed on his forehead. He had to curb a nervous impulse to use his rifle on the advance guards.

The Indians came closer to the rock formation and gestured to each other that everything looked normal. To Levi's relief, they went to the bank of the river where both of them leaned against a clump of beech trees and looked back on the trail. A few minutes later, the main party came into view and proceeded to the edge of the water, preparing to place the canoes into the river. They seemed secure that they were undetected, or else one of the scouts would have checked the rim of the outcrop.

Four more Indians and a man in a long black robe entered the depression below Levi and his two companions. They were half carrying and half dragging three canoes piled with baggage and supplies. At the tail end of the column, four white captives, two of them very frightened women, were closely guarded by two more armed Indians. Then, Levi spotted two small children six or seven years old walking with the women. The presence of a small boy and a girl made their task even more difficult.

What were they to do? It was a time when Levi's inexperience bothered him. He felt responsible for the safe retrieval of the six captives. Eight armed men and the priest against the three bordermen gave him pause. Levi crawled back from the rim of the ledge motioning for the other two to come closer. He assigned Angus and John to take out the two rear guards with their rifles while he concentrated on one of the four Indians with the canoes. With hand signals and barely discernable whispers, he instructed them to drop their rifles after they had been fired; grab their two pistols and leap from the ledge so as to insert themselves between the captives and their guards. For a brief moment their eyes met. They understood the danger and approved of Levi's hastily contrived plan of action. Each carried a knife strapped to their right legs and a tomahawk on their belts.

Slowly the three bordermen raised their rifles, confident that at such a short range they could take down three of the enemy below. Levi had been nervous and uncertain until the moment he raised the rifle to his shoulder. Then, a calm resolve steadied his strong arms as he set his sights on the tallest Indian to his right. Three triggers were pulled in unison. A click of the hammer being released, a puff of smoke from the powder pan, and the deadly charged lead bullets were sent to their targets.

They dropped from their secure perch to the ground below screaming to the top of their lungs for the captives to run south along the water's edge. The prisoners were quick to obey the command as they stepped over the three dead bodies and fled the scene. The priest and remaining Indians took flight, unsure how many men had attacked them. One paused to raise his musket. Angus saw him and was the first to fire his pistol, knocking the Indian down with blood pumping from his mouth. The two Indians that had been in the vanguard rapidly sped out of sight, leaving only two that had been carrying the canoes to react to the priest's demand. It was too close quarters for them to use their muskets. In a wild frenzy the two drew their tomahawks and charged. The attacking Abenaki were stopped with two shots from pistols held by Levi and John.

Levi and his companions now had one loaded and charged pistol each in case the scouts decided to return. He immediately ordered John and Angus to pursue the fleeing Indians far enough that they were satisfied they would not return to harm the captives. Levi confronted the apoplectic priest with a raised and cocked pistol hoping that the black-robed white man would make a threatening move towards him so that he could pull the trigger in self-defense. He hated the religious fanatics more than he did the Indians. He did not look upon them as men of God, instead he saw them as cheerleaders who incited their flock of natives to greater and more ruthless behavior against their enemies. They were murderous men filled with hatred and vile contempt for the English Protestants.

The priest looked first at the barrel of the raised pistol then into Levi's eyes where he saw hatred equal to his own. The sneer quickly disappeared from his lips. Levi told him to raise his hands and clasp the back of his head. The Jesuit appeared insulted and did not comply with the curt request.

"I don't know if you speak or understand English, but I warn you, black-robe, one false move and I'll take delight in sending you to hell where you belong."

"I understand you very well, young man," the priest quickly replied.

Levi checked each fallen body and was satisfied that they were all dead. "Now, Jesuit, you lie down on the ground on your stomach with arms and legs spread wide. Move, you contemptible excuse for a human being!"

The priest arrogantly took his time to comply. It triggered a response from Levi that filled his eyes with fear. "Do it now, you coward, or I'll take great pleasure in scalping you just to hear you scream and give you something to remember me by."

The priest kneeled down and positioned himself in front of Levi. A large knife fell from his robes. Levi dragged the knife closer to the priest's hand with his foot and taunted him, surprised at his own ruthlessness.

"Why don't you go for your knife, Jesuit? By the way, how many are in your party?"

As expected, the priest remained silent. Levi stepped on the knife beside the priest and hollered for the captives to return to the canoes. "We can cross the river now. Come quickly while the area is still safe. Do not be afraid. They cannot harm you anymore."

The two women were the first to come into view, breathing heavily. The two men followed in their footsteps carrying one each of the children. The older of the men approached Levi.

"Thank God you came. I'm Todd Tanner," he cried emotionally. He was a muscular Scot with a booming voice, cradling one of the children in his arms. He examined the inert bodies scattered on the ground and handed the little girl to one of the women. "Here, Mother, ye can give thanks the Lord answered our prayers."

"We must empty the canoes as fast as we can and pass over to the other side to safety," Levi replied, helping them remove the supplies. "Can you two men take them across the river?"

"Yes, we can," answered the younger of the two men. "I'm Morley Tanner. This is my father, mother, sister, and brother. The animals killed one of my brothers while we were at the village. The priest screamed something to the Abenaki and they instantly killed him with a tomahawk to the head for no reason at all. They surprised us before we could defend ourselves."

Todd Tanner saw that the priest was still alive and bent over to pick him up off the ground. "Stand up and look me in the eye you beast who hides behind a robe like a woman."

Levi made a step to intervene. One of the women grabbed him by the arm to restrain him. The powerful Todd Tanner was in search of justice, and Levi let the drama play out. Tanner saw the knife on the ground and picked it up, backing the priest to a large hemlock tree near the water's edge. Filled with rage, the Scot picked the priest a foot off the ground and held him against the tree. Then, he drove the knife into his stomach with such force that it penetrated the tree trunk several inches. It was deep enough that it held the priest's body pinned against the tree suspended off the ground. The priest's eyes bulged with fear, and loud screams passed his lips loudly at first, tapering off to a low gurgle as blood belched from his mouth.

Levi saw what was happening and refused to judge Tanner's motivation for the act. It was a scene of retribution that he never forgot.

Todd Tanner slowly turned to Levi, and in a calm voice assured him that he and his son could get them across the river with no problem. Levi suggested that they hurry. He pushed the filled canoes into deep water and watched them reach the eastern shore where Captain Stevens and some British soldiers were waiting for them.

"Well," Levi turned to John and Angus, pointing to the priest. "The angry Scot extracted justice for his loss. We'll leave the executed priest behind as a message to those who may follow in his footsteps. Hopefully those who got away will spread the word that there is a force in the field that intends to resist their bloody tactics. What do you think?"

"I've been thinking the same thing, but we've got to be cautious and alert. This may enrage them to seek revenge instead of quell their raids," Angus answered, feeling nauseous. The priest hung on the side of the tree with his head touching his chest.

The three men loaded and primed their firearms and climbed into the saddle, intent on further pursuit of the fleeing Indians. John was by far the best tracker in the company. He located the tracks and followed a short way on foot before mounting his horse. They followed the tracks about three miles north until John spotted one of the Indians on a ridge ahead of them running parallel to the river. They threw caution to the wind and pursued the two Indians at a fast pace, hoping that they would alert the Indians. Levi loudly spoke to the men that they should stop at a convenient location where they could take a parting shot at the two renegades. That opportunity presented itself with a clear view of the panting Indians. Angus took aim with his rifle and fired. One of the Indians dropped to the ground, leaving his companion unharmed so that he could spread the word about what took place.

An hour later, they reigned in at Fort Number Four. Levi suggested that John and Angus replenish their supplies in preparation of a prolonged patrol into the northern reaches of the New Hampshire Grants. Captain Stevens had escorted the exhausted captives into the great room above the main entrance of the fort.

The Tanner family were newcomers to the area, having come from Londonderry seeking land nearby on the Connecticut River. Levi checked on the family to see how they were doing and for a report on just how the abduction took place within the shadow of the fort. It was a disturbing incident. As he engaged the Tanner family about what took place, Morley, the young son told him that a friend by the name of Thomas Ryan was on his way to the fort so that they could homestead as neighbors and increase their protection against attacks.

Levi told them about young Daniel Ryan, wondering if there could be some relation. The name struck Morley like a physical blow. "Yes... yes, I know the family. Daniel's father was Tom's brother. We all left Ireland on the same ship. Where is the lad?"

Chapter Nine

Captain Stevens had been present when Levi told the Tanner family about Daniel Ryan. The Tanners were pleased when Captain Stevens ordered the next supply convoy from Portsmouth to bring the child to the fort, certain that it would be safe for the child, for the trains were generally well protected.

Conditions on the frontier were very unsettled, demanding vigilance and caution. Raids were a daily occurrence within his area of responsibility. Concern for the few brave souls who had ventured into the wilderness to claim their lands was the reason that Captain Stevens requested Levi to conduct a scouting reconnaissance into the northern Connecticut River region known as the Upper Coos. Levi, John, and Angus agreed to the assignment and spent two weeks exploring and scouting the area, taking precautions to avoid any confrontation with the numerous bands of roaming Abenaki and their French companions that they encountered. They ranged from the Upper Coos to the rugged mountainous range to the east as far as the headwaters of the Merrimack River. The heavy concentration of armed bodies of Indians and French soldiers was significant. They returned to Number Four to report the activity to Captain Stevens, who was not surprised. John returned to New Boston with a supply wagon train with the information about the Coos patrol.

The fort was a busy staging location for supplies on their way to the Hudson Valley region. The constant flow of supply trains to and from the fort brought valuable information to Captain Stevens. When Levi and Angus reported to him about the conditions they had found in the northern frontier, he became concerned about a delegation of men empowered to purchase the release of several individuals captured from the frontier region north of Portsmouth.

* * *

Colonel Levi Wilson recalled that eight-week patrol with vivid images that had not diminished over time. The party had left Portsmouth and arrived at Fort Number Four just as Levi and Angus had completed their report to Captain Stevens. They were helping themselves to some hot venison stew in the great room above the entrance to the fort when Levi saw Captain Stevens searching for him in the limited light.

Levi was concerned with the sober look on the Captain's face. "Is anything wrong?"

"I'm glad to see that you've not left the fort, Levi," Captain Stevens accepted a hot mug of tea from one of the men tending the fire in the great room. "An unusual situation has developed, and I hate to ask you and Angus for another favor..."

"What can we do, Sir?" Levi knew that the Captain never asked for favors unless it was urgent.

Captain Stevens told Levi and Angus about the capture and death of several men and women, and that the Abenaki and French were asking for a sizeable ransom for their safe return. "The message from the Saint Francis tribe in Odanak has assured me that a ransom party will have safe passage to and from the fort. I'm asking you and Angus to accompany the delegates under a white flag to complete the transaction. I know it's asking a lot of you, but I have nobody else available."

"How do you know they'll honor the white flag?" Angus had anxiously asked.

"The messenger from the village is a Christian whom I personally know. I believe they will keep their word. It's in their best interest to honor the protocol because it's very profitable for them," Captain Stevens had told them.

Levi turned to Angus, "What do you think, Angus?"

Angus hunched his shoulders and replied, "I'll join you, Levi. It will be a long journey though."

"Okay, Captain. We'll take on the task, but when we return, both of us have got to return to New Boston," Levi assured Captain Stevens.

"I knew I could count on you two. Thanks," he answered, turning to outfit the expedition as soon as possible.

The two hundred mile trek north was traversed without incident. They traveled up the Connecticut to its headwaters, then northwesterly over mountainous terrain to the St. Francis River, where they were met by a scout party of Abenaki who guided them to the village at Odanak on the Saint Lawrence River.

The negotiations took place the moment they arrived. The delegates did not bring enough gold coins with them to meet the demands of the Abenaki council. Levi and the delegates told the council chiefs that they wanted to retrieve all of the white captives and would return with additional money by late fall. The council was reluctant to trust such an arrangement and suggested that they leave one hostage at Odanak until the additional money was delivered.

The delegates argued forcefully against the suggestion. Levi was worried that the entire swap was about to be dismissed by some members of the council. The hostages were discouraged, and one of the women began to cry uncontrollably. Angus had been a silent spectator who had volunteered to stay with the Indians, provided all of the captives went free. A priest that sat with the council liked that idea, and they agreed.

Angus handed Levi the reigns to his horse and smiled. "Well, Levi. Hurry back before winter sets in, and don't worry, I'll be just fine."

It was a courageous act, and Levi was moved. "You take care, Angus. Don't do anything to anger them. I promise, I'll return with the money for your release as quickly as possible."

One of the three women was given Angus's horse for the trip back to the fort. The ransomed party of seven adults was the largest group ever exchanged while Captain Stevens was commander of Fort Number Four. On the return trip, Levi had relinquished his mount to two of the women who were weakened by their ordeal. Levi led the party back to the fort on foot, impatient with their slow progress.

The day they arrived at the junction of the Connecticut and Ammonoosuc Rivers was cold and rainy with strong winds blowing out of the north. The women in their charge were physically and emotionally spent, so Levi suggested that they stop to build some sort of shelter and start a fire. He sent out two hunting parties for some fresh meat. Later that afternoon,

Captain Stevens, with an advance group of four soldiers, rode into their camp.

Encouraged by the additional manpower, Levi had argued forcefully for permission to leave the party and push on to the fort where he could obtain the money for Angus's release. Captain Stevens agreed with him and wished him good luck. Levi left all the food and blankets he had on his Narragansett and rode for ten hours nonstop to the fort, arriving completely exhausted. He reported to the lieutenant in charge and informed him that Stevens wanted a relief squad sent up the east bank of the river to guide the party back to the fort.

Levi wearily crawled into a bear robe and slept soundly for six hours. He was awakened by the sound of musketry on the east shore near the great meadow. Quickly gathering his rifle, Levi ran downstairs to the stockade where his horse was already saddled and was being fed and watered by one of the soldiers. He checked the priming of his rifle and inserted it in the scabbard on his saddle.

The soldier saw him and said, "My lieutenant told me to feed and water your horse. I placed a bag of pemmican over the saddle horn. He said that you wanted to leave just as soon as you woke up."

"Thanks, Sergeant. Did the lieutenant give you anything else for me?"

"Yes, Sir. He instructed me to hang on to this purse of gold coins and give it to you, personally. There are a lot of scoundrels out there who would do anything to steal it from you, Lieutenant."

"It looks as if you've thought of everything, Sergeant. Has a relief column been sent out to Captain Stevens?"

"A boat filled with supplies and an escort left at dawn, Sir," the burly sergeant replied, handing him a canteen of water.

Levi was anxious to get back on the trail to Odanak. "Thanks for everything, Sergeant. Now, if you'll open the gate, I'll be on my way."

Levi rode hard for three hours over a well-beaten path on the east bank of the river, pushing the gallant Narragansett to her limits. He was concerned about Angus's safety and was anxious to complete the ransom transaction. He caught up with the relief column near the collection of cabins at the Lebanon trading post. He paused to give the horse a rest and enjoy a hot mug of tea. The sergeant in charge of the column questioned him about the captives, explaining the approximate location of the group and that if the column kept close to the river bank they would intercept the party.

"We can't travel as fast as you can, Lieutenant," the sergeant told him. "The boat is much slower than our column, and I don't dare to leave them unprotected."

"That sounds like a sound policy, Sergeant. Thanks for the vittles and drink." Levi climbed back into his saddle. "I'll let them know that you're on your way with all possible haste."

Two hours after leaving the relief column, Levi was riding at a canter along a wooded track, watching the immediate ground ahead of him instead of the surrounding territory for any sign of trouble. The path led to a high ledge on his right. His instincts told him it was a good spot for an ambush, yet his concern for speed overruled his instinct for safety. Without warning, a young Indian warrior leaped off the ledge above him, knocking Levi out of the saddle. The horse stopped a short distance from the two struggling men.

They landed on the ground, knocking the wind out of Levi. The Indian was on top of him. Desperately trying to breathe, Levi defended himself, hitting the man several times on the side of the head. He was angry at himself. His own violation of the principles of scouting or traveling in Indian Territory made him angrier at himself than his ferocious opponent. The Indian was able to land several hard blows against his chest and face while Levi remained motionless a few seconds to regain his equilibrium.

Covering his head with his arms, Levi realized that the attacker had no other weapon than his fists. Then, the attacker was turning him over so as to reach the knife Levi always wore in his right legging. He knew then that he was in mortal danger and with all the strength he possessed, Levi rolled away and grasped the knife in his right hand. Lying on the ground, he swung the knife in several wide arcs towards the Indian. It was a desperate act of survival. Suddenly, the silent wilderness was filled with loud cries of pain.

Levi leaped to his feet, prepared to deliver the fatal stroke to his assailant. To his surprise, the young Indian was doubled up, lying on the ground holding onto his stomach. The Narragansett was close to the struggle, and Levi's first instinct propelled him to the saddle to leave the area. Then he realized how young his attacker was, maybe fourteen or fifteen, and quickly dismounted to assist the youth. He grasped the boy's body and rolled him onto his back so that he could see how badly he was wounded. The boy stared at Levi, filled with terror that he was about to die, and refused to be still on the ground.

"Do you understand English?" Levi asked in a clear, distinct tone.

There was no response from the boy, except for a shaking of his head as if he did not understand. Levi pulled the youth's doe hunting shirt up over the wound in order to determine its gravity. His knife was razor-sharp and he had succeeded in making a cut about six inches across the belly toward his right side just below the rib cage. The cut was about a half to a quarter inch deep and was bleeding profusely. Levi breathed a sigh of relief. It was not a stab wound as he expected.

Holding the boy on the ground, Levi motioned to him that he wanted to get something out of his saddle bag. The youth seemed to understand that Levi wanted to help him and remained still. The wound needed to be cleaned, and all he had was a small flask of rum. He offered the boy a drink from it, but he refused, turning his head away. In that moment, Levi poured a liberal amount of rum across the cut, enlisting a scream from the boy. Soon the burning sensation subsided, and Levi took one of his cleanest blankets and sliced off several strips so that he could bind the wound.

The Indian saw what Levi was going to do and helped by holding one end of the long strip of blanket while it was being wound tightly around the wound to promote clotting of the blood. Otherwise the boy would bleed to death. The Indian had a haggard, unkempt look about him. His clothing was torn and soiled, and his moccasins were worn through. Once the wound was tended to, Levi lifted the satchel of pemmican off the saddle and offered it to the boy. His eyes opened wide and he began to ravenously eat the nourishing mixture.

Levi smiled at him and went to the river to fill his canteen. For ten minutes the boy ate and drank until he was satisfied and returned the satchel to him. Levi kneeled down on the ground and smoothed out a section of the forest floor. Pointing to the Connecticut River, Levi drew a line in the soil. The boy shook his head as if he understood. Continuing the line on the ground, Levi drew another line from the northeast, indicating the Ammonoosuc junction with the Connecticut. Again the boy seemed to comprehend what he was drawing. Pointing to himself and the boy, Levi then drew a dotted line from the rivers to the northwest. It took several gestures for Levi to communicate that he was going to the Odanak village.

The knowledge that Levi was going to the village drew a smile from the boy. He weighed about a hundred and twenty pounds, so Levi believed that the Narragansett could carry double if he was not pushed too hard. He helped the boy onto the horse behind the saddle and then climbed aboard. A couple of hours later, they entered the region locally known as the Upper Coos. Levi was familiar with it from his most recent scouting of the area. It was a traditional fishing and agricultural area for several different tribes of woodland Indians in the northeast.

Levi cautiously took one of his pistols from its holster and tucked it in his belt. He estimated that Captain Stevens's party was miles further to the north of the Upper Coos. The trail was well-worn from generations of constant usage, and Levi was uncomfortable being so vulnerable. He felt the boy tense behind him and stopped to check the surrounding territory with his telescope. The scarlet coat of a British soldier brought a sigh of relief to his lips. Levi recognized Captain Stevens ahead, and rode the Narragansett into the friendly encampment.

A large fire was burning with dozens of large split and cleaned salmon and whitefish drying and smoking over the green hardwood branches. Captain Stevens greeted him warmly. "My young friend, you have made remarkable time. My scout on yonder ridge saw you coming miles away. Who is your young passenger?"

Captain Stevens could speak several of the native dialects, and walked up to help the Indian climb down, talking to him at the same time.

"I ran into him a few miles back on the trail. He's alone and doesn't understand English," Levi replied.

The youth told Captain Stevens in a halting manner, that he was a Penobscot Indian and had accompanied a hunting party into the great mountains. Several encounters with English settlers had thinned their ranks until he was alone with only two others. They eventually died of an illness, probably smallpox, leaving him alone and a long way from his native village. Stevens told Levi that the Penobscot were a much more docile tribe than the Abenaki, but once aroused, they could be equally brutal and tenacious.

"The boy told me that their party had visited Benacour on the Saint Lawrence River. I informed him that it was for the best for him to continue to Odanak with you. There is much trade between the various tribes that the boy will have no trouble getting back to his people. He also related that several Delaware were also in the original hunting party," Captain Stevens said, watching the youth with interest.

"Is he in agreement with your suggestion, Captain?"

"Levi," the Captain smiled and grasped him by the shoulder. "You have found a friend in this young warrior. He claims you could have killed him; instead, you bound his wounds. I'd say that you've got a good companion for the trek to Odanak. He should help insure a safe passage for you two through the frontier."

Captain Stevens had the boy follow him so that he could properly dress the wound with clean linens. While that was taking place, Levi located Angus's horse and had it prepared for the young Indian. They ate their fill of fresh fish and within an hour, were again on the trail, leaving the river plain, heading cross country to the northwest. Levi estimated that they had three more hours of daylight left before they made camp for the night.

The campsite was beside a clear running brook, and Levi tethered the horses so that they could drink and moisten their hooves. There was a small patch of marsh grass available for them to graze. After hobbling the horses, Levi directed his companion, whom he had nicknamed "Jo-Jo", to take two of the blankets and a bearskin to sleep on. They did not want to build a fire and ate pemmican before retiring to the welcome blankets. Both were dead tired.

Levi collected his two pistols and his carbine, placing them under the blanket to keep dry. That night he had thought of home and the family he left behind. At times he was homesick for the warmth and supportive atmosphere that reigned in the Wilson home. It was a source of strength for him, and, on occasion, during the past weeks he had questioned his ability to maintain such an intense operation he had so enthusiastically endorsed and committed himself to lead.

He was exhausted; yet, for him, sleep did not come easy in the wilderness. He looked to see if the young Penobscot, Jo-Jo, had settled down. The young Indian had stayed close to Levi throughout the day, and had placed his bear skin next to him with their feet facing the northwest. It was the first time that Levi had had a chance to observe a Native American over a period of time. Jo-Jo had chiseled facial features with high cheek bones and a copper complexion. Once he realized that Levi was not an enemy, he relaxed and even laughed when Levi had passed under a branch, pushing it aside. Jo-Jo was too close, and it slapped him in the face, causing him to cry out in his native tongue.

Levi had apologized, and they both laughed over the incident. It was a simple thing, but a bond had been established and it made Levi feel good. In that moment of discovery, Levi saw Jo-Jo stand a little taller and projected himself in a proud, regal air. It was the first time that Levi had ever thought of the native population as something more than an enemy.

The next morning, Levi was shaken by Jo-Jo who placed a hand over his mouth. It startled Levi until his eyes became accustomed to the limited light, and he saw Jo-Jo point at an opening in the forest below their campsite. He saw several figures, which he assumed were Abenaki, and grabbed his carbine. Jo-Jo restrained him and began rolling up his bedroll, motioning that they quietly leave the area. It seemed to be a logical maneuver. Levi had taken his advice, gathered his belongings, and secured them on the horse. They soon left the area, making a wide circle around the Abenaki camp.

An hour later, they paused to eat some smoked fish that Captain Stevens had given them. Levi was appreciative of the way Jo-Jo had handled a situation that could have been deadly for him. He tried to convey the fact that they had become friends by placing his hand over his heart and touching Jo-Jo's chest. He smiled and nodded to confirm the gesture.

Late that same day they had passed a lookout point at the entrance to the St. Francis village high on the bank of the St. Francis River. Shortly, Levi and Jo-Jo were met by a number of warriors who escorted them to the council tent, where they joined Angus. He appeared to be well-treated. They slept in the same tipi, anxious to conclude their transaction that next morning.

The next morning, true to their word, the Abenaki and the French priest, who spoke some English, counted out the twelve gold coins Levi had been given at Number Four. The priest and council members seemed pleased. The priest told them that they were free to leave the village and would be granted safe passage back to the fort as long as they carried the white flag. The priest promised that Jo-Jo would be returned to his people. Jo-Jo was the only son of a very prominent Penobscot chief who would also be told of Levi's compassion for the young man.

Just as they were ready to leave, Levi gave Jo-Jo a handshake and a hug and told him, "I wish you well and a long life, my friend."

To Levi's astonishment, Jo-Jo replied in understandable English, "Thank you for your kind words, Lieutenant Wilson."

Chapter Ten

Fort Niagara, October 1781

Colonel Levi Wilson accepted a hot mug of tea from a Continental soldier. "Thank you, young man," he said, noting the youth in the limited light of the early evening. "There's a nip in the air, and the tea with a spot of rum will warm my weary bones."

"The British commander suggested that you should come inside, Sir," the soldier replied, handing him a great coat. "In case you chose to remain alone out here, he told me to bring you this coat."

"I'm not used to being pampered so much. Thanks for the kind thought, soldier. Now that the war is over, memories and thoughts of the long struggle have consumed me. For the first time in many years, old faces and images of trying and difficult times flow through my thoughts like a river after a spring thaw. By the way, where are you from, lad?"

"I'm Private Daniel Marion, Colonel. I'm from Portsmouth, New Hampshire. I was captured by the British this last summer. I served with General Sullivan when he mounted his expedition against the Iroquois Indians and their white plunderers."

"Portsmouth men are of good stock, son. Your neighbors and brothers have helped to lead the way to our victory. Thank you for the hot toddy and the great coat. I can understand that the British higher command are unhappy with the turn of events, but the men in the ranks seem to be pleased that the guns are silent. I think all soldiers share that relief. The merriment that is taking place in the mess hall is an indication that peace is welcome by our former enemy combatants. The night is young, and one of my favorite pastimes is reflecting on the length of the journey that has brought us to this day."

"I understand, Colonel," the guard said and turned to leave.

"By the way, Private, what is the status of the continental soldiers held here at Fort Niagara? Are you now free to leave?"

"The British detachment here at the fort have treated us with respect and fed us the same rations as their own garrison," Private Marion told him. "They have about twenty American prisoners here, and they will be glad to see us leave. Food and supplies are scarce, especially since the large number of refugee Indians have arrived at the fort, a result of General Sullivan's successful campaign to the west."

"Perhaps you, and any other prisoner, can leave with me and my contingent of scouts. The war is over, and our services are no longer needed. We begin our journey home with great expectations and a prayer of thanksgiving that we've been spared the fate of so many fine men, British and American. Tell the commandant that we appreciate his gracious hospitality and that we will be leaving in the morning."

"Yes, Sir. I'll be happy to join your party and share your sentiments. Goodnight, Sir."

"You'll be most welcome, son," replied Levi, pulling the heavy coat over his shoulders and warming his large bony hands around the hot mug. Once again, he returned to the early days when the New Hampshire Border Company was his first command.

* * *

It was October of 1754, and Levi had not been home all summer, except for two hurried trips to replenish food and ammunition, since he had left in May. Four long, grueling months wandering the northern frontier had completely exhausted him and the rest of the company. A warm bed and good food was badly needed and was most welcome. He had slept for twenty-two hours that first day, awaking in his familiar bed looking at the dark shadows of the twin mountains to the east of their home. It was night, and a full harvest moon lit up the landscape.

He quietly made his way down the stairs to the kitchen where Beth was placing a log on the fire. He glanced at the large clock on the mantel. It was midnight.

"Good Lord, I haven't slept like that for a long time."

"Your mother and father retired hours ago," Beth explained, avoiding his searching eyes. "I offered to keep the fires going in case you awoke and wanted something to eat."

"That's thoughtful of you," Levi had said. He took a seat at the large kitchen table. "Say, is that fresh bread that I smell?"

"Yes," she smiled, placing a large loaf of oatmeal bread and a long knife on the table in front of him. "I took it out of the oven an hour ago. Would you like some tea? There's a fresh pot on the grill. I was going to have some before I turned in for the night."

"Oh, yes, Beth. That would be a treat for me. Would you, by chance, have any molasses to accompany the bread?"

"Your mother told me that you had a fondness for bread and molasses. She said it was your 'sweet tooth'. There's always a supply of molasses on the farm. Your father makes his own rum, or grog, as he calls it."

"Well, I like the molasses better than the grog."

Beth poured two tins of hot tea from the heavy kettle suspended over the grill, and then placed a small bowl of molasses on the table for him. She seemed apprehensive and uncomfortable. Levi had correctly attributed it to her advance state of pregnancy, so he brought the subject up.

"You're looking good, Beth. My father always said that women have a very special glow about them when they are carrying another life inside their body. It is becoming to you, Beth."

She again avoided his eyes and quietly sipped her tea. "The truth is, I feel uncomfortable and awkward. Your mother has been very kind and supportive of my decision to carry the child. I agonized over that decision for a long time."

Levi saw her anguish and replied calmly, "Ever since the time we carried you from your cabin, I've tried to place myself in your position so that I could better appreciate the trauma you have been suffering. But, alas, I can never know, Beth. No one can ever know unless they also experience the same thing under the same set of circumstances. I'm proud of you, and believe you've made the right decision."

"Even after all the atrocities you've witnessed, you can still think that way?" Tears filled her eyes, clouding her vision. "There are times when I think that I made a mistake. The child will be a half-breed, neither white nor Indian, and he or she will be shunned by both societies. I could unwisely be giving birth to a child who will know nothing but unhappiness and discontent. Those thoughts trouble me every hour of the day. Your family has been wonderful, and I am so thankful for their support of my decision. I try to earn my keep and be worthy of their compassion, but doubts and worries about the future cloud my rational thinking. There are times when I think I should have killed myself."

Frightened by what she said, Levi grasped her hands across the table and held them. "That kind of language scares me, Beth. It had to be God's will that spared you from the atrocities that killed your husband. That very same thought came to me as we were riding away from the burning cabin. There's already too much death and despair taking place on our frontier, and the Abenaki are not the only perpetrators of such misdeeds."

"Your words help, Levi, but they do not displace the fact that my child has already been the object of hatred. There have been times when the seed that was planted by a barbaric savage has been a source of hatred and loathsome thoughts. The child has already been robbed of the basic legacies a normal child is endowed with even before birth. Most children come into this world into a home filled with love, joy, and great expectations. I have denied that to my child..." Large tears filled her eyes. Beth turned from the table to face the fireplace, consumed with despair and shame. She wept openly, wiping away the tears with her apron.

Levi felt ill-equipped to console her. She spoke of issues he had not thought of, and it made him feel inadequate. "I don't know what to say, Beth. If I had the power to erase all of those ugly images and bad thoughts from your mind, I'd do it, but I'm at a loss for words to comfort you. I, for one, will never judge you for a condition that you were powerless to prevent. Perhaps you are blessed with the pregnancy because God knows you have the courage and strength to nurture one of his chosen children. You have earned my family's respect and affection by your modest and generous disposition. How lucky a child is to have you for a mother! We are judged by what is in our hearts, and you should remember that when those bad thoughts visit you."

Beth had stopped her convulsive cries of despair and placed another log on the glowing coals of the fire. That evening, she and Levi had become friends. They had reached a level of intimacy that both of them found comforting. The ability to share deeply-held thoughts without being judged or questioned was the building of a foundation of trust and fellowship that enriched both of their lives.

Levi frequently thought of Beth, especially during the long, lonely vigils around a campfire in the middle of a wilderness. The loneliness he had always felt when darkness accompanied the silent hush that only a wilderness is capable of creating, turned his thoughts inward. It was easy then to reflect on those things closest to his heart. He honestly admitted that when he was with Beth he was content and at ease. Each journey away from home triggered an awareness that made him uncomfortable. He was never one to deceive himself — he had fallen in love with Beth!

In the beginning, he wasn't certain if it was because of her unfortunate condition or in spite of it. Less than a year had passed since the loss of her husband, yet he still felt responsible for her welfare. Remembering the depth of her sorrow and anguish at what she had to endure, it was easy for him to involuntarily maintain the role of protector. The day she had threatened to kill herself and her baby frightened him.

Beth had instinctively sensed the feelings he harbored, and it helped her to make the decision to bear the child she was carrying. The Wilson family had opened their hearts and hearth to her with sincerity and compassion. How lucky she was! She was never certain if her attraction to Levi was the result of having been saved from a horrible death, or if it was honest recognition of his decent and gentle ways. She worried for his safety when he was not home. A bond of friendship had begun on that very first day when she felt safe and secure in his strong arms.

Maude Wilson looked after Beth and her condition as if she was one of her own. Beth blossomed into a beautiful expectant mother, comfortable with the decision she had made. One day in the middle of a raging northeaster snowstorm, an anxious and troubled Beth gave birth to a healthy seven pound baby girl whom she named Naomi. Maude and two other midwives assisted Beth. The instant the crying baby was placed in her arms to be nursed, all the doubts and anticipation about her acceptance of the child disappeared. The fact that she had brought forth a unique human being, the product of her womb, gave her a proud sense of achievement and empowerment.

Little Naomi was over a month old when Levi saw her for the first time. The memory still brought a smile to his lips. He had been on expeditions west of the Connecticut River all summer and fall and was looking forward to a winter of rest and recuperation. He needed the healing powers of home more and more as the years passed. His body ached from bitter cold and damp nights lying on a deerskin waiting for dawn to come. The patrols were becoming more and more discouraging. For every life and settler's cabin saved from destruction, two were being obliterated; yet, they doggedly continued their effort to secure the frontier. At times Levi questioned the feasibility of obtaining security even with a large armed force.

Levi had returned home late in the evening when everyone had gone to bed except for Beth who was sitting in a rocking chair nursing Naomi in the kitchen in front of a crackling fire. He spotted her through the window on the east side of the house on his way to the barn, where he fed and watered the faithful Narragansett. He quietly approached the kitchen door gently knocking to announce himself.

The sudden knock at the door alarmed Beth, turning away to cover herself. "Who is it?" she asked in a strained voice.

"Don't be alarmed, Beth. It's me, Levi." He dropped his heavy deerskin bag beside the door. "I saw you as I rode by. I pushed hard to get here before darkness, but it was not possible. The snow is beginning to add up. Ah, how good the fire feels." He knelt to throw another log on the heavy bed of red coals, and turned to look at Beth and the baby. It took a while for his eyes to become accustomed to the flickering shadows in the kitchen.

Beth modestly fastened the front of her dress before confronting him. She barely recognized him with his long beard and unkempt hair. He smelled of wood smoke and gunpowder and his deep-set eyes alarmed her. She caught her breath and smiled at him.

"Your folks will be relieved to learn that their son has come home. How nice it is to see you, Levi. This is my daughter." She held Naomi up in front of her near the light from the fire.

Naomi's dark eyes and black hair were much like Beth's. The baby's complexion was lighter than he expected. She was fast asleep in her mother's arms. One small hand grasped Beth's dress. His first thought was that she was like a miniature adult. He was fascinated by her small fingers with dimples at the joints and miniature perfect nails. How tiny and helpless she appeared!

"She's beautiful, Beth. What's her name?"

"I called her Naomi which comes from Hebrew, meaning 'my delight'. My mother was Jewish, and my father was Irish. It was my mother who taught me to read and write English. Her family were devoted Jews, and that is one of the reasons my husband's family disapproved of me and our marriage. Like I told you months ago, my parents are dead. Eric still has family somewhere out there, but they never welcomed us into their family circle." She watched Levi for some reaction to her ancestry, anxious to determine what he thought.

Levi knew that she was testing him. He paused to collect his thoughts before answering. "Little Naomi is an adorable baby. Such perfect little fingers and arms. She is blessed to have you for a mother, Beth. The fact that you are Jewish from your mother is interesting, but actually, the source of our ancestry is not as important as the virtues that guide our lives. We should be judged by what is in our hearts, not by some arbitrary standard that others apply to us."

She heard what he was saying, and the tightness around her eyes and mouth softened. It was the kind of answer she had expected from Levi. "You are a generous person, Levi Wilson. Not everyone thinks like that."

"May I hold the baby?" he asked with outstretched arms.

"Here, why don't you sit in the rocker and relax. She loves to be rocked. I fear I've already begun to spoil her," Beth laughed softly, placing Naomi in his arms and began preparing some hot tea for him.

Naomi woke up when he took her, and stared at his beard. She reached to touch it and pulled away uncertain about it. He felt her tiny body tighten, aware that she was in the arms of a stranger. Levi felt a sudden sense of empowerment come over him. How fragile and innocent she was! He began to slowly rock in the chair, watching her go from a wide awake baby to a drowsy, relaxing state, and then, finally, to a sound sleep. He felt her relax in his arms and was amused at the way she struggled to keep her eyes open and ultimately gave in to sleep with every muscle in her body relaxed. Levi was intoxicated by the precious little human being that fell asleep in his strong arms without a whimper. From that moment, he was determined to protect and shelter her from harm, with his life if that was what it took.

Beth busied herself placing bread, cheese, and honey along with his hot tea on the table. She went into the small pantry off to the right of the fireplace for a small apple pie.

"This was a good year for the apple crop. Your father told me it was the biggest one yet. You must be starved, Levi."

He smiled at her. "Food that I don't have to prepare is always welcome. It's good to be home, Beth. You're looking good. Motherhood is becoming to you."

She blushed at his compliment and turned away from him to hide a tear that gathered in her left eye. Levi saw the sudden change and asked, "What's wrong, Beth. If I've said something out of turn, I apologize. I'm sorry."

"No," she cried, still turned away from him. "I was only thinking that we've talked about everything except that which has ruled my life for the past ten months. What are your real thoughts about Naomi? She's half white and half Abenaki. I followed your advice and that of your dear mother to have this child that was conceived in a brutal act of terror and bestiality. At some point during my pregnancy that fact became unimportant, because the child I felt within my body was a real part of me, and I was giving it a life. The sacredness of that life has influenced every thought I have towards her; yet, I know that it has nothing to do with how others perceive her. It's important to me to know precisely how you feel about the whole situation. I've cried myself to sleep countless nights trying to accept my condition. I've been able to put those ugly thoughts behind me. My only worry was how you would handle it. I love Naomi with all my heart, possibly more than would be normal, because she needs to be protected against the bigotry and ignorance of those who cannot accept her."

"It's strange that you should mention protection, Beth. I was just having similar thoughts about this little girl who has fallen asleep in the arms of a stranger; yet, she felt secure enough to give in to her natural instincts. It has touched me, and I can honestly admit to you, Beth, that I will never have a word or a thought towards her or her mother regarding the circumstances of her conception. You were chosen to bring Naomi into this world, and I'm so proud of both of you."

Blinded by tears of joy, Beth took Naomi from Levi and placed her in the cradle beside the fireplace. She turned to Levi who held out his arms to her. She came into them and gently laid her head against his chest.

"I've fallen in love with you, Beth."

Tears of happiness flowed down her cheeks. "I love you, too."

She lifted her lips to him, and in that moment of discovery, they faced the world as one. Later that spring, they were married, and little Naomi became a Wilson in name and spirit.

* * *

The war with the French and their Indian allies had in reality been underway for years before it was formally declared when a young and inexperienced Colonel George Washington of the Virginia militia ambushed a detachment of French soldiers in the Ohio Valley. The infamous deed ignited the fury that had already been present on the frontier. Levi's small detachment of New Hampshire Border Company men had been in operation for years when the incident in the Ohio Valley unleashed a new wave of debauchery and violence. Governor Wentworth recognized the need for additional policing of the frontier and authorized the formation of a ranger regiment under the command of Robert Rogers from Starkstown.

Levi knew Rogers, who was promoted to the rank of colonel. The rangers had a much broader mandate than the Border Company. Rogers spent hours conferring with Levi about the training, supplying, and control of a military formation that operated on the periphery of military customs and traditions. Levi looked upon his company as a constabulary unit instead of a military formation. He also had some reservations about Robert Rogers that he kept to himself. Time would validate his suspicions to be correct, but the turbulent frontier was well served by the rangers who performed spectacular feats of physical endurance and courage heralded by those who witnessed their tenacity and effectiveness in the wilderness environment.

Governor Shirley of Massachusetts and Governor Wentworth of New Hampshire were both interested in the upper Coos region of the Connecticut River where it meets the Ammonoosuc River. It was a rich and fertile valley, a natural location for a fort to be built by the British who were anxious to lay their claim to the region. Several exploratory missions were sent to the region. Some even began to cut a roadway to connect the Merrimack River with the Connecticut River.

Levi and his Border Company continued to lead excursions into the region and had accompanied Captain Stevens on several expeditions to ransom captives at the Odanak village on the Saint Francis River. On one such transaction, Levi was accompanied by Angus Campbell and John Thompson escorting a family consisting of mother, father, and two young girls ages ten and fourteen years back to Rumford. Levi and Captain Stevens had successfully conducted their exchange. They made their way to the Connecticut where Stevens and his aide continued down the river to Number Four.

Levi was leading his party, mounted on two horses, with Angus and John securing their flanks at about two hundred yards distance. A few miles after bidding Stevens good-bye, Levi and the distraught family, without warning, rode straight into an Indian encampment with six warriors and a French officer. Neither Angus nor John had picked up any signs of their presence. It was a surprise to both parties.

The two girls and mother became hysterical and out of control when they recognized their predicament. Levi instantly ascertained that resistance would be fatal for himself and the family, so, with his limited knowledge of the language, he boldly greeted the members of the camp. The Indians were drying venison over a fire, and he asked if he and his party might share some of their food. The ruse worked!

Hospitality is a natural part of the woodland Indian tradition. They helped the family dismount even though the women were distraught and frightened. They were offered strips of venison. It tasted good to Levi who had not eaten all day. They had given away all of their food as part of the ransom cost of the family. The French soldier was a young lieutenant of the French marines. He remained silent while Levi and the others ate the offered venison with relish. Levi became uncomfortable with his interest and was contemplating just

93

how he was going to disengage himself and the family from their predicament. He was concerned about Angus and John, hoping that they would keep their distance and remain out of sight.

After Levi had satisfied his hunger with the venison, he rose from the fire and began to shake hands with each member of the Indian band. The move surprised the warriors and they enthusiastically participated in the handshake ritual. Levi repeated, "thank you" over and over to each warrior.

Turning to the French officer, Levi said, "Thank you for your hospitality, Lieutenant. Merci, merci, bon ami," and held out his hand.

The officer accepted it and smiled. "I speak some English, Lieutenant. I understand that you have just returned from Saint Francis village. Tell the family in your care that you may continue on your way without fear. This band will not harm you."

"Please convey our appreciation for their generous sharing of food," Levi replied with a silent prayer of thanksgiving.

"Your appreciation is already acknowledged by them. Incidentally, your two companions on the flanks are waiting for you," the officer told him with a knowing smile.

Startled by the statement, Levi replied, "We must be on our way now." He motioned to the family to get ready to leave and helped the mother and daughters onto the horses.

Levi quickly climbed into the saddle, feeling more secure with his pistols within reach. He was baffled by the friendly treatment and was afraid it might suddenly turn deadly.

The French officer approached Levi and asked, "Are you the one known as Lieutenant Wilson of the New Hampshire Border Company?"

"Yes, I'm Lieutenant Wilson," Levi boldly answered.

"I have heard of you from a Penobscot friend, who has asked that you always be given safe passage."

"And who is this Penobscot you speak of, Lieutenant?"

The French marine smiled again. "He told me that you had called him 'Jo-Jo'. Not all of the native people are savages. He and I had attended the missionary school. I can tell you that the French have no plans to build a fort on the upper Connecticut River. Take that message to your superiors. I am afraid that much blood will be shed before the struggle for land is settled.

94

Both you and I are intruders upon land which the natives have considered sacred for hundreds of years. We must never lose sight of that fact, but the weak will always be overpowered by the stronger combatant. It is nature's way."

"You speak with a wise tongue, Lieutenant," Levi responded to the eloquence of the French marine. "In time, the native tribes will be the vanquished people, and the British and/or French will eventually rule the land. Right or wrong, that is a fact."

"Go in peace, Lieutenant Wilson. Your reputation as a fair man has preceded you, and in this instance has saved your scalp."

"For that, I'm grateful. Au revoir, Lieutenant."

Chapter Eleven

Fort Niagara, October 1781

Young Lieutenant Angus Campbell cautiously returned to the location where Colonel Levi Wilson was resting under a large white pine tree overlooking the turbulent Niagara River empty into Lake Ontario. The soft moonlight rays of the harvest moon reflected off the water. The rugged peaks of the western mountains were highlighted by the moonlight, casting shadows against the glistening waters. It was a peaceful scene that soothed Levi's troubled soul.

The young officer was twenty-six years old and had been assigned to Levi's scout detachment by General John Sullivan, a long-standing friend to Levi. Angus was hesitant to interrupt the Colonel's solitude and approached him with quiet steps in case he was sleeping.

"I hear someone nearby," announced Levi. "Declare yourself!"

"It's me, Lieutenant Campbell, Sir."

"Well, never try to sneak up on me from behind. It's a good way to get yourself shot. What can I do for you?" Angus did not see that the Colonel's rifled carbine was cocked and ready to fire. Old habits of the trail are never abandoned.

"I apologize for the intrusion, Sir. Ever since I was assigned to your detachment to escort the Indians to Fort Niagara, I've been wondering a lot about my father. I know that he served with you until his death, and was wondering if you could tell me how he died. I never knew."

Levi studied Angus's shadow and invited him to sit for a spell. "Your father was a dear friend for many years. We shared the hardships of countless trails all across the frontier

96

wilderness. Your father was a big man in a small wiry frame of sinew and muscle. If you're half the man your father was, you'll be lucky, son. When he was on watch, I could sleep with ease knowing that he was there. You were born a short time after he was killed. That was twenty-seven years ago, and I remember it as if it was yesterday."

Angus detected sadness in his colonel's voice, and listened with rapt attention. Angus, Sr., had been one of the original ranger volunteers of the New Hampshire Border Company and was a strong supporter of its policing function. The frontier had been a most dangerous place then. Both the white men and the Indians tenaciously defended their lands. The matter was resolved ultimately by overwhelming numbers of new settlers pushing deeper and deeper into lands used by the Abenaki for hunting and fishing. The Border Company was responsible for saving many lives over the years.

The conflict between France and England had been raging on the western frontier for decades. It became a more serious conflict when George Washington ignited the spark between the two nations vying for control of the continent. Levi and his border company were sent to the Lake Champlain-Hudson River corridor to assist the Colonial forces under General William Johnson, the former Indian Agent for New York. The atmosphere was tense with each side building forts and encampments as quickly as men and materials became available.

General Johnson wanted to build a fort at the southern end of Lake George and was collecting his forces. He had won a stunning victory against the French forces at Lake George, where he paused to plan his next move against the strongly fortified Fort Carillon at the southern end of Lake Champlain.

Levi had arrived in the area and reported to General Johnson with six men including Angus and John. They were ordered to determine the strength and location of the French around Fort Carillon. It was a vast area of wilderness, and they were in the field for weeks at a time, monitoring events at the huge French stronghold. They duly observed and reported arrivals and departures of men and material from the fort and accurately mapped the ground defenses outside of the fortress walls.

One day Angus was leading a patrol of three men near the portage between Lake Champlain and Lake George when they stumbled onto a French work force building a sawmill. Angus was killed in the first exchange of fire. The French force greatly outnumbered the scouts, so they quickly left the area, as they were trained to do, leaving the body of their companion and friend where he fell. Levi later learned that the French garrison had given Angus a Christian burial with military honors. His body remains at the fort's cemetery.

"As far as I know your father was killed instantly in the first volley from the French. Now that the war with the British is over, perhaps you and your family will be able to remove his remains from Fort Ticonderoga. Personally, I would leave them where he fell. He was a courageous soldier and a passionate patriot, loved by all who knew him. I've thought of him every day since his death with a deep sense of loss. I'm sure that his spirit is at peace and is proud that his sacrifice helped to make our victory possible. Your father is one of countless hundreds of fine men who willingly gave their all in the cause of freedom and liberty, and who will always remain unknown and unsung except for those of us who mourn their loss."

Angus Campbell, Jr., was hearing the words for the first time. He never knew his father. "I appreciate your sentiments, Colonel."

"My friend, Angus, holds a special place in my heart. He was one of my responsibilities, and I lost him for all of us. That's about all I can tell you, Lieutenant."

Angus stood to leave and turned toward Levi, "Is there anything I can get for you, Colonel?"

"Get a good night's sleep, Lieutenant. Tomorrow will be a tiring day. Once we head for home, we'll give the mounts their head."

"Goodnight, Sir."

The evening air was cooling, but Levi did not notice the change. He had bedded down more nights under the stars than he had in his own bed. The retelling of Angus's death brought to mind two other losses that still bothered him – Captain Stevens and John Thompson. The tall, slender Thompson was a gentle man with nerves of steel. He had served Levi and the Border Company with loyalty and courage. He was killed at

Fort William Henry. General Johnson built the structure at the tip of Lake George.

Once the fort was completed, it became a source of irritation to the French and their Indian allies. Levi stopped by the fort after a long circuitous patrol with four scouts. They were low on food and ammunition and needed to be resupplied. Gathering of intelligence on the enemy was an on-going operation that changed everyday. Levi and his men frequently escorted supply wagons to and from Fort Number Four.

Saint Patrick's Day, the spring of 1757, was still etched in Levi's memory. Several hundred French and Indian troops with a large contingent of artillery on sleds, had attacked the fort across the frozen lake in the early morning hours prior to sunrise. The bulk of the garrison force were of Scotch-Irish descent. They traditionally celebrated their patron saint with lavish amounts of rum. Over three-quarters of the men were drunk. The only troops available to man the ramparts were a number of rangers commanded by Captain John Stark and Levi's few scouts. Stark and Levi had agreed the night before the attack that they had to limit the amount of rum, so they ordered the sutler to lock up the rum until authorized by Stark, who retired early.

Levi had recognized the potential crisis ahead and had sent John and one other scout outside of the walls to determine if there was any enemy presence nearby. Four hours later, John and his companion returned with a report that shocked Stark and Levi. Over five hundred men, half of them French marines with large caliber cannons, were just beyond range of the fort artillery. They warned the commandant and immediately rushed every ranger and scout to the north walls with a large supply of ammunition and powder. They were their first line of defense.

Fires could be seen burning at the artillery emplacements, and Stark cautioned the few sober artillerymen to fix their sights on those positions and to load their cannons with maximum powder charges. It was imperative that those French cannons be put out of commission when the order to fire was given. The rest of the men on the north wall were cautioned to hold their fire until the enemy ranks were within range of their muskets. Each man was instructed to aim below the white belts the French marines fastened around their waists.

The enemy was under the assumption that the garrison would be sleeping off their heavy consumption of rum; therefore, they were advancing as quietly as possible with ladders to breach the walls. Levi and Stark were watching in the limited light, hoping that the front ranks would continue closer to their deadly rifled carbines and muskets.

Even today, Levi recalled proudly how well they had performed. Their marksmanship and rapid-fire techniques took a heavy toll of the French lines. Huge gaps developed after the first volley. His Border Company was placing about fifteen aimed shots per minute into the French ranks. After several minutes of sustained fire, they ceased firing to clean and cool their weapons. It was a display of discipline and extraordinary marksmanship.

The French artillery began their bombardment about the same time as the fort's gunners touched the fire hole of their weapons. Several of the French weapons were taken out in that first barrage, but those that remained were able to smash through the stockade wall in two locations. The artillery duel lasted for about a half an hour until the British gunners were able to locate the remaining French pieces and eliminate them. During the bombardment, John Thompson was killed instantly by a cannon ball that almost cut him in half.

Levi saw the breached stockade walls and told the commander that he was going to remove his four men from the defense line and place them in a position where they could deny the enemy access through the ruptured wall. It was at that time that Levi had noted John's lifeless body draped over splintered pieces of wood. The four men quickly constructed a defensive position out of bags of flour strewed all over the ground in front of the breached wall. They had prepared their pistols for any last minute emergency. Levi had been especially proud of the continuous fire which his men poured into the attacking French infantry, denying them access to the broken stockade fence.

The battle lasted for an hour. Dead and wounded French soldiers and marines were piled high in front of the breach, but the withering fire from the four bordermen maintained the integrity of the wall. After wave upon wave of attacking echelons, the French commander broke off the assault and retreated north across the ice. Later, the border company pursued the withdrawing troops to make sure they were not grouping for another assault. They found hundreds of holes chopped into the ice by the defeated French. They had buried their dead comrades in the cold waters of Lake George!

Over the years that spanned the two conflicts in which Levi had fought, he had served under several commanders. Some were mediocre, and some were outstanding. A few had been outright incompetent. He judged his peers not on their social standing, but on their success on the battlefield and for their selfless dedication and compassion for the men placed in their care. Few leaders could compare to the sturdy frontiersman from New Hampshire, General John Stark. Levi admired the man for his modest and unpretentious ways, and for his unequalled ability to inspire troops to their full capacity. The troops who served with him would have stormed the gates of Hell if he had asked them. He suffered the losses in silence. His gruff exterior could not hide the depth of his sorrow. His deep-set eyes always had that far-away-look that registered the horror of combat. He was a soldier's soldier, ferocious in combat and compassionate and caring for friend and foe alike when the guns were silent.

Another New Hampshire man, General John Sullivan, was a brave leader who had recently conducted a successful campaign against the Six Nation Confederacy who had been terrorizing settlements along the New York–Pennsylvania frontier. Levi's bordermen had scouted several weeks for the general. Sullivan's army had conducted a scorched-earth policy against the confederacy, destroying several communities and winter's supplies of food. Levi had no trouble punishing those who committed atrocities, but he refused to fight women and children. Consequently, he had informed Sullivan that he and his men were leaving. Winter quarters in the wilderness had little appeal to him, and he yearned to return to his home in New Boston.

* * *

On their way to New Hampshire, his small band of bordermen had escorted a hundred captive Wyandot Indians to Fort Niagara where the commander, Colonel Raymond Howe, had given them food and shelter from his dwindling stocks.

Levi liked the young British officer and apologized for leading the refugee Indians to his command.

"I was reluctant to enter your fort even with the white flag. I'm glad that you honored it, Colonel. I've had the distinction, if it can be called that, of visiting every fortified installation on the western frontier with one exception, Fort Niagara."

"Well," the young Colonel Howe anxiously greeted him, "I recently took command of this facility. I know that my predecessors have been responsible for unleashing grievous acts of barbarism against your people."

Levi evaluated the British colonel with penetrating eyes and replied simply, "You're correct, Colonel, and I've spent most of my life trying to counteract such behavior on the frontier. It is time for it to end, or we will all perish in our pursuit of justice and vengeance. Do I have your permission to rest my small band of bordermen for the night? We plan to leave in the morning – destination, New Hampshire."

"Your reputation has preceded you, Colonel Wilson. I, too, share your Scotch-Irish ancestry. Quarters will be provided for you and your men. You are a guest, not a prisoner. I will be honored if you would share my table with me tonight."

"It will be my pleasure. I thank you for your hospitality, Sir." With that, Levi left the large headquarters building and sought a quiet place to rest his weary body and to reflect on where he had been and where he was going.

Later, a familiar voice called Levi from the distance. "Colonel Wilson, this is Lieutenant Campbell, again. Colonel Howe requests your presence at his quarters. You and I have been invited to dine with our former enemies."

"The offer is gratefully accepted, Angus. I don't know about you, but I'm anxious to sit down to a meal prepared by someone besides you or me," Levi replied.

"Follow me, Sir. I've just come from his headquarters. There's a chill in the air."

"Aye, and it's only the beginning. October warns us to prepare for the coming months of winter. I'm anxious to return to New Hampshire, but in all honesty, I'll miss these large lakes and swift-running streams. I understand now why so many settlers abandoned their rocky, hillside farms of New England for the rich soils of the Champlain and Ohio valley regions."

The two bordermen entered the small building adjacent to the massive barracks. Two British sentries came to attention as they drew near the entrance. It was an act of respect, yet Levi felt strange. Just a few hours ago the soldiers were his enemies. Now, they were simply soldiers doing their duty at a lonely outpost on the frontier. An orderly opened the door for them to enter a large room with an open ceiling and two large fireplaces at opposite ends of the room.

"Ah, here are our honored guests," Colonel Howe announced, walking briskly towards them. He was a small man with angular features and a thin physique. He had an authoritative air, but his request for Levi and Angus to dine with him was sincere and gracious. "Welcome, Colonel Wilson and Lieutenant Campbell. You may place your weapons on the table beside the west fireplace."

"We accept your hospitality in the spirit it is given, Colonel Howe," Levi replied, removing his doeskin jacket and ammunition belt and standing with his back to the crackling fire. "These old bones can absorb a lot of heat. It has been a long time since I ate a meal sheltered from the weather and set at a table filled with such a variety of fine foods."

"I understand how you feel, Colonel Wilson. Hopefully, breaking bread together will help put to rest all the pain and suffering that this war has caused. Wars between brothers are always the most vicious. I'm relieved that it's over."

Levi scrutinized his host while he was speaking. In any other time or place, he would have been pleased to call him a friend. "I join you, Colonel Howe, in making a toast for a lasting peace. I'm also relieved that the killing is over. In the same breath, I must admit that I will have a difficult time erasing from my mind sights and sounds of the atrocities against helpless settlers and their families. The nerve center of operations in the Mohawk Valley of New York, the Wyoming Valley of Pennsylvania, and the new settlements in Kentucky were Fort Detroit and Fort Niagara."

"I cannot deny your charge, Colonel Wilson. I, personally, was opposed to such atrocities." the British Colonel paused when he met Levi's stare. "I am also a soldier who must obey orders, and it is a matter of record that my opposition to the use of native troops to conduct guerilla warfare against a civilian population was the reason I was sent to Fort Louisburg in Nova

Scotia. I heartily applaud your valiant attempts to bring peace to a terrorized region of this new world, and I can understand why your famous General Sullivan is now conducting his scorched-earth campaign against those tribes responsible for the reign of terror, but I still am opposed to some of the tactics he is using against them."

Levi smiled at his host. "Colonel, we agree on more issues than we disagree. The settlers, the Indians, and the land speculators all have different visions for this new land's future, and each vision was based on retaining or acquiring land that other people occupied or wanted. It's time for the two major combatants to look for common ground on issues and to not lose sight of the fact that we share a common heritage of culture and language. Acknowledgment of those facts should contribute to a lasting and fair peace."

"You are a wise man, Colonel Wilson. May that joining together in common cause begin now with our toast and prayer for what you call a lasting and a fair peace."

Levi and Angus raised their wine glasses in unison with their British brothers.

Chapter Twelve

Levi's last evening at Fort Niagara was a pleasant respite from his normal routine. Colonel Howe proved himself to be a gracious host, considering that the two men were enemy combatants a short time before. Several Continental Army prisoners were also present. They were hoping for an early release so that they could return to their families before heavy snows settled in for the winter.

Colonel Howe had offered to Levi and his men the use of a supply boat to transport them to the eastern shore of Lake Ontario. It was now unloading supplies for Niagara.

Levi pondered the offer. "Under normal circumstances, we would be pleased to be transported one hundred and fifty miles closer to home, but we can make better time with our horses, Colonel. Use the space for the transfer and repatriation of your prisoners. All of us in my small band are anxious to make the journey as quickly as possible."

"I would feel the same way, Colonel Wilson," the gracious British officer remarked with a puzzled look on his face. "I have been wondering all evening about you. One of the officers confided in me about a young lady that you rescued from an Abenaki attack which killed her husband. Two years later, this young Captain purchased the homestead and told me that the husband's name was Eric Baker. This Eric Baker interests me."

The name startled Levi, and he turned from the snapping fire to confront Colonel Howe. "The incident with the Bakers took place when I was a very young man. May I ask how this Eric Baker interests you?"

Colonel Howe was visibly moved by the mention of the names, and solemnly told Levi that he had an older brother named Eric Baker. They had the same mother, but Eric's father,

Eric, Senior, was killed in a coal mine accident. Months after his death, their mother married a distant cousin of Admiral Richard Howe. When Eric, Jr., was about twelve years old, he was indentured to a family who left Scotland and was never heard from again. Colonel Howe was keenly interested in anything that might clear up the mystery of what happened to his brother. He had red hair and was missing a finger on his left hand, the result of an accident splitting wood.

Levi thought back to that time and place when he buried Beth's husband. "I remember that the man had red hair. He had been scalped, but his sideburns were carrot red. I cannot recall if he had a finger missing or not." Levi stared at the flickering flames and remembered how it had been so many years ago. "Those were frightening times, and I admit that I was scared to death when we buried Eric Baker's remains. I was more observant of the surrounding forest than I was of the butchered man's body."

"I understand, Colonel." Colonel Howe shook his head from side to side. "Could you describe where he is buried? I don't mean now, but sometime when you arrive home could you send me a map of his gravesite? It would mean a lot to me to visit it someday. Eric was my only brother. My dear mother died never knowing where he was or what he was doing. I thank you for having this conversation with me, Colonel Wilson."

Levi grasped the British officer by the shoulders and looked into his eyes. "Colonel Howe, you have triggered memories that have remained buried for years. I'll be pleased to draw you a map and will consider it an honor to escort you to Eric's final resting place at any time you chose to make the trip. Now, I want to thank you for your gracious hospitality. Lieutenant Campbell and I have a long journey ahead of us, and we must excuse ourselves for the evening."

Levi and Angus shook hands with those present and retired to the second floor of the large barracks building where they shared a room with two British officers. Levi laid down on a straw-filled pallet and closed his eyes. He was weary and physically spent, but he could not sleep. Memories filled his head to overflowing. He smiled. Beth had called them "echoes from the past".

The ten year period after the massacre of Beth's husband was a time when the frontier exploded with violence. Long before the beginning of the French and Indian War, Levi had rapidly grown from an idealistic young man to a very seasoned adult who had seen just about every type of atrocity the wily Indians and their resourceful French companions were capable of performing on human beings. Once the butchery was experienced, it created a lust for revenge and justice, hardening many individuals to rationalize that any form of retribution was never enough.

Fear and hatred ruled the wilderness; yet, hardy individuals in search of their dreams were propelled into the dark forest, confident in their ability to bring the dream to fruition. Those were harsh years for Levi and his Border Company. Year after year, they took to the forest that stretched from the Merrimack River to the Hudson River, trying to bring some kind of security to the chaos that prevailed.

It was common practice for both sides to go into winter quarters when the winter snows became too difficult for travel. It was a time when peace settled over the land, and isolated settlers breathed easier. Families drew closer together and sometimes laughter could be heard inside the snow-covered cabins.

Levi enjoyed those months the most. Body and soul needed to be nurtured and healed in preparation for the cycle that started all over again in the spring. Each year passed and was pretty much the same, but there were significant milestones along the way that he frequently recalled with a mixture of sadness and happiness. Foremost in his reverie were the images he held dear of the gentle Beth Baker who had been raped by her husband's murderers, leaving her pregnant.

Levi had returned to the farm the winter the child was born. His parents had opened their hearts and their hearth to the mild-mannered Beth. She felt comfortable with the Wilson family and was determined to do her share of work while she carried the child. Her decision to have the child and care for it after birth was a heroic move that met with the approval of the Wilson family. She blossomed into a beautiful mother-to-be. A calm confidence radiated from her that was noticed by all who met her.

She was kind and thoughtful and most appreciative to the Wilson family for their hospitality. Levi had fallen in love with her. He kept his feelings to himself because he thought that it was too soon for such a serious declaration of affection. Besides, he was not sure if he was influenced with pity for her condition or if it was just an infatuation.

He had not been around many girls his age except for his neighbor, Abigail Campbell, Angus's sister. One day when they were about eight years old, he had kissed her on the cheek while they were walking home from school. She was surprised and asked him if he really liked her.

He was shy and replied, "I think you're pretty, Abigail."

"Do you think I'm the prettiest girl you've ever seen?"

"Yes," he confessed, "I've always thought so."

"Does that mean that you will marry me when we get older?"

He had to think about that question. His spontaneous kiss had developed into a very uncomfortable situation. "You mean like my mother and father and your parents?"

"Of course. Are you too shy to tell me?"

"No, I just hadn't thought about it, Abigail. Probably when we grow up we'll be two different people."

She jumped to conclusions and got mad. "Levi Wilson, you're just scared to tell me the truth. Don't try to kiss me again." She then skipped ahead of him and ran home.

It was an innocent time in their lives, and from that moment, both assumed that they would be married when they grew up. As the years went by, Levi matured into a very serious young man, while Abigail grew prettier and prettier with her auburn red hair. Young men were drawn to her, and she was anxious to show Levi that she could have any man she wanted. She became obsessed with her looks. He ceased to enjoy her company because she had to be the center of attention, and he did not like selfish people. She also had a fiery temper that was most unbecoming to a young lady.

During that same winter that Beth gave birth to her daughter, Naomi, Abigail pulled into the yard with a horse and sleigh. Levi was grooming one of the horses in the barn and walked out to greet her.

"Hi, Abigail, it's nice to see you."

"My, Levi, Father tells me what you're doing out there in the frontier. We've been worried about your safety," she exclaimed, warmly embracing him.

Levi was uncomfortable with her show of possessiveness and modestly explained, "We hope that our small force has made a difference. It was exciting, and I'm glad to be home." He had attached the horse weight to the mare's halter and escorted her into the house.

Beth was quietly nursing Naomi beside the snapping kitchen fireplace. She quickly turned away from the visitors and covered herself. The baby cried briefly for more milk, but Beth placed her on her left shoulder to burp her. Levi felt awkward intruding on such a personal moment.

"I'm sorry, Beth. I didn't realize that you were nursing the baby."

Beth replied with a nervous tremor in her voice, "The kitchen is the warmest room in the house."

"This is our neighbor, Abigail Campbell. She stopped by for a visit. Abigail, this is Beth Baker."

"I apologize for my untimely visit. I was anxious to see Levi. He has had all of us worried with his long journeys in the forest. How old is the baby?" Abigail asked, removing a scarf from her head.

"Naomi is two months old." Beth cradled her in her arms in a gentle rocking motion. "She's a good baby and doesn't cry much. Her name means 'my delight' in Hebrew. The Wilson family has been very kind to us and we are thankful for their generosity."

Levi leaned over Naomi and gently brushed a lock of hair from her face. "She's a beautiful child who smiles most of the time."

"Would you like to hold her, Abigail?" Beth asked.

Abigail stepped away from Beth and exclaimed in a strained voice, "Heavens no, not with an Indian baby!"

The words struck Beth like a heavy blow. She quickly turned away to hide her face from Levi and Abigail, angry, hurt, and offended by the outburst.

Levi reacted instantly. "Abigail, how could you say that? Little Naomi is a beautiful baby."

Abigail was apologetic with her reaction to the dark-skinned baby. "I'm sorry, I did not mean to offend you, Beth.

It's just that what we've been experiencing from the dreaded Abenaki, I associate all Indians the same way. I'm sorry..."

Beth gently placed Naomi in her crib beside the fireplace and slowly confronted Abigail with tears bursting for release. "Your apology is accepted. I brought this child into the world knowing full well that some people who have experienced the brutality of the Abenaki would hate her for what she is. Maybe I was wrong to carry her to birth. Tell me, Abigail, what would you have done if it had happened to you?"

Levi looked at Abigail for her response. She looked at him and then at Beth with wild angry eyes and blurted her answer in a wavering voice. "I can tell you one thing, I would never allow it to happen. I would kill myself first."

Beth shook her head, remembering how it had been. "While the sordid act was taking place and afterwards, I wanted to die, and I would have done so with ease, but a strange thing happened to me. I had prayed to God to strike me dead, and when that did not take place, I began to feel empowered to be the child's mother, and I have fortified myself to do just that. If the child offends your self-imposed sense of superiority, Miss Abigail, you can simply go to hell." Beth calmly picked up Naomi and left the room.

"You were right, Beth," Levi called to her. "All of us have supported your courageous decision."

"Well, if that's the way things are, I'm sorry I came by, Levi."

"What did you expect Beth to do, agree with you? You don't know her like we do. She's a kind, hardworking person who has shown a lot of courage. Few would be able to do what she has chosen to do, and I will always be her friend and defend her decision. My family is proud of her."

"Yes, that is evident, Levi," Abigail replied curtly. "You do what you want. Don't bother to see me out; I know my way."

The confrontation left him confused and angry, but most of all, it left him concerned about Beth's feelings. He felt responsible for the flare-up because he had brought Abigail into the house. He quickly went into the large sitting room off the kitchen where Beth was rocking Naomi to sleep. Not wanting to disturb her, Levi bent over Beth and gently wiped away the tears on her cheeks.

"Do not let ones like Abigail judge you, Beth," he whispered in her ear. "She's unworthy, and we are proud of you."

She lifted her eyes and softly replied, "Thank you for the support."

He left the house and continued with his chores in the barn, filled with emotions and not quite sure what this episode had accomplished. Twenty minutes later, Beth walked into the barn with a shawl over her shoulders and a white bonnet covering her head.

"Levi," she said, standing in front of him in a hesitant voice. "I'm sorry if I placed you in a position that caused a difference of opinion between you and Abigail. I do not want any trouble from her or anyone else, and I apologize for being curt and rude to her. After all, she has been your friend for years, and I'm really still a stranger."

Levi heard her conciliatory words and smiled. There was something hauntingly lovely about this young lady that touched him, and he explained about Abigail. "You have nothing to be sorry for, Beth. Abigail should have apologized to you for her remark. She can be a snob. There are times when she thinks she owns me, and I hate that about her. We've been friends since childhood. There is nothing more, and I've reminded her of that fact occasionally."

"She's very pretty with her long blonde curls."

"Maybe she is," Levi shrugged his shoulders. "I use a different set of values to define people."

"Thank you for telling me that." Beth smiled at him and turned to leave the barn.

"Beth," he called out to her. She turned to look into his eyes and ran into his open arms. He embraced her and kissed her waiting lips. She responded, clasping her arms around his neck, and began to cry.

"No more tears, Beth."

It was a powerful moment of discovery for both of them. His world was never the same after that embrace. A few months later they were married. Those years together were the happiest of his life. She and little Naomi had brought order and meaning to his existence. He loved them and cared for them when the dreaded smallpox invaded their paradise. Beth and the baby had contracted it at the same time. He stood over them day and night, trying to counteract the high fever that eventually consumed Beth and little Naomi, a day later.

Levi could not think about the early years without feeling the pain of their deaths. His world had been shattered, and he had lost his way. He had taken to the wilderness like a man gone mad, unable to shake the despair that was consuming him. He spent a winter patrolling the northern reaches of the New Hampshire Grants with no plans or order to his rambling.

One night in the midst of a snowstorm high in the mountains, he lay wrapped in a bear skin with a foot of snow covering him. He was cold and had given up hope and was indifferent to his perilous position in the dead of winter. Beth and Naomi were always on his mind, and he was ready to give up the strife to join them. The night was ending, and a beautiful red sun appeared in the East, suppressing the violent swirling snow. The silence was so powerful that it awoke him, and he swept the bearskin off him in a circular motion.

The first thing he saw was the sunrise. It blinded him with its brilliance. The cold penetrated him as he quickly kicked the snow away from the campfire of the night before. There were no coals left to ignite a new fire. Though he had been functioning in a vacuum, Levi had adhered to the long-ingrained habits of wilderness travel by collecting enough dry firewood for the night. Blowing on his cold mittens, he stepped to a nearby balsam fir tree and snapped off an armful of small dry branches and ripped off some bark from a nearby white birch tree. Then he prepared a small conical-shaped supply of dead branches with some white birch in the center of it. The pistol he always carried in his belt was already primed with gunpowder. He cocked the pistol, and, holding a finger over the ignition hole, sprinkled the powder from the pan over the small pile of twigs and pulled the trigger. Instantly, a small flame leaped from the branches, and soon, a roaring fire was snapping and crackling beneath his small pot of water and a few tea leaves. The warmth that flowed from the fire was like a friend. It invigorated his sluggish body. He had sat for a long time staring at the flames. Suddenly, he saw a shadowy image of Beth's face looking at him. It was so real that he had reached out to her and called her name.

He was afraid that he was going mad, yet he could see her image now with clarity even though wisps of smoke stung his

112

eyes. Her lips began to move, and he dropped to his knees when he heard her speak in that soft voice that never failed to touch him: "Do not be sad, my beloved, I will always be with you." Then, she was gone.

In that moment, he felt a soft breeze caress his face, and he wept until there were no more tears to fall.

Chapter Thirteen

October 1781 Fort Niagara

The fall winds blew fiercely across the dark blue waters of Lake Ontario, kicking up waves four feet high. Levi looked out the barracks window to the West and saw the restless water churning. It was still dark, but there was enough light to reflect the highlights of the water cascading from the tops of the waves. Habits cultivated from years of scouting on the wilderness frontier always awoke him before the approaching dawn. It was the quietest part of the day when he could make plans and solve problems. These interludes of solitude were important for his emotional stability.

Now that the British were no longer an adversary, the threat of attack from that source was no longer a factor. The most dangerous element on the frontier were the thieves, outlaws, and scoundrels that preyed on helpless victims. September and October were months when all of the northern Indian tribes were busy hunting for food to last them through the winter months.

Levi's Border Company had frequent contact with the Abenaki tribes in the area. They had faithfully served with them in patrolling the area. Their neutral stance during the war of revolution was rigidly enforced, and they "watched the forests" to see which of the combatants would win the contest. They were interested in preserving their way of life, and Levi had become one of their most ardent supporters when a few years earlier, he had been a bitter enemy.

Watching the thrashing lake outside, Levi was glad that he had refused a boat trip to Fort Oswego. Garrison troops were beginning to stir, and he picked up the welcome aroma of tea being brewed over a fire. He gently shook Angus from a sound sleep and left the barrack room for the mess hall on the first floor of the building. His four border men had beat him to the serving line. Angus showed up with a sheepish grin on his face. Breakfast consisted of fresh lake salmon, oatmeal, and hot tea. All of the men ate heartily to fortify themselves for the day ahead of them. As soon as they finished their meal, Levi instructed the men to get their mounts ready for the long trek home. He left the mess facility to locate Colonel Howe, recognizing him beside the horse corral.

"Good morning, Colonel Howe. We're preparing to vacate your fort shortly. Your generous contribution to our food supply is appreciated."

"You're welcome, Colonel." The commandant looked drawn and worried.

"Is there anything wrong, Colonel?" Levi confronted him.

"Late last night, several boats tied up at our dock and unloaded over a hundred Indian refugees fleeing from General John Sullivan's division that is sweeping the Mohawk Valley region in an effort to curb the terrorist elements. The Indians and others seeking asylum here at the fort really worry me."

"I recently left Sullivan's command, as you already know. He was ordered to stop the terror that had spread across the land, and he's doing it. I refuse to condemn him, but I do take issue with some of his tactics, and I'm not surprised that you are seeing an increase in refugees."

Colonel Howe nodded his head gravely and told him, "I can honestly confide in you that we just do not have enough supplies to maintain such a large population of refugees. My main British sources are no longer available to me, and hunting parties are finding game scarce within several miles of the fort. Our main food supply will have to be the lake, but I did not intend to burden you with my problem. As a matter of fact, I have a favor to ask of you."

"I'd be glad to help if I can," Levi replied, detecting a troubled look in Colonel Howe's dark eyes.

"Some of the individuals that landed last night had been visiting relatives in Canada. They are Chippewa, Delaware, and some Abenaki. They wish to return to the Lake Champlain region and have requested assistance to make the long journey.

There are about fifteen people in the group, including four or five children."

"You don't ask for much, do you, Colonel?" Levi was concerned that a party with children traveling hundreds of miles during winter time could be a disaster. "Do they have any horses, or do they intend to walk?"

Angus saw the two colonels having a serious conversation and approached them. "Is there anything wrong?"

Levi described the situation to him and continued, "Under the circumstances, we can't refuse their request, but the reality of what is ahead of us demands that we have supplies and horses to transport such a group. If they are left on foot, they will never make it, and that is a fact you must agree with, Colonel."

The overwhelmed British colonel scanned the dark waters of the lake as if he was seeking some magic solution to his dilemma. "These are desperate times and I cannot deny your stark reality. I can give you six horses and two wagons for supplies and for carrying the children and women. I will do what I can for food, but my resources are meager."

Levi felt sorry for the predicament in which Colonel Howe found himself. "I sympathize for you, Colonel. I will escort the people to the Hudson or Lake Champlain with the wagons and horses you can provide. I have one more request, Sir. My contingent have enough blankets and furs to keep warm, but I want you to provide enough blankets and/or furs for the refugees. Without protection against a severe winter, it would be suicide for the group, and I will not accept the responsibility unless you can supply those items."

Colonel Howe turned to Levi and smiled. "The things you ask for will be provided. The party is now being fed in the barracks. I can have the horses, wagons, and supplies ready in one hour."

"It's a blustery morning, and I'll feel better if we head out parallel to Lake Ontario as soon as you can, Colonel Howe. Time is precious. Angus, prepare the men for escort duty. We'll proceed with two riders out on each flank and one on the point as usual. The main source of trouble as I see it will be bandits and thieves who are taking advantage of the lack of security forces throughout the northern wilderness. While you are seeing to that duty, I would like to meet with the people who will accompany us on the eastern track to home."

The fort's mess facilities were being pushed to the maximum. The place was jammed with people sitting, standing, and waiting for a chance to be served. Colonel Howe asked Levi to wait for him at the door to the mess hall. A few minutes later, he returned with several Indians all dressed in hunting shirts and doeskin pants. He saw them and had second thoughts about his promise to the commandant.

"They have already eaten and are anxious to be on their way. Come, let's get away from this noisy place. We can go over to the corral and talk without distraction."

Levi fell in step with Colonel Howe when a small Indian boy of about eight or nine years ran to his side and grasped his hand. "Well, young man, are you going on a long journey with us?"

The child answered in English, "I go back home with you."

Before Levi could acknowledge his reply, a woman with long black air with streaks of gray done up on two long braids, grabbed the boy's other hand and firmly reprimanded him. "Now, James, be respectful to the man. When I tell you to be quiet, you must be quiet, do you understand?"

Levi released the boy's hand. "He's not a bother, lady. You two speak English very well. Very few natives are able to. I was apprehensive about communicating with your people because my ability to speak in any of the Algonquin dialects is limited at best."

"Many of this tribe speak English. We went to the mission school at Memphremagog," the lady shyly told him. "James is my grandson. His mother and father both became sick and died last summer."

"Why are you so far from the mission school at this time of year?" Levi questioned her.

Before she could answer him, Colonel Howe spoke to him. "Colonel Wilson, this lady with the little boy is the spokesperson for the band of Indians. She has already told them that you are willing to act as guide and escort to the Hudson River. Now, we can supply you with some food, but we are very limited, and you'll have to supplement your needs with game and fish along the way. I have promised Colonel Wilson two

117

wagons to carry the women, children, and supplies and six horses in total.

"You people should be prepared for a long and difficult journey, but you will be better off than if you stayed here at the fort where we are dangerously low on food, firewood, and medicine. My troops will outfit the horses and wagons immediately. I know that Colonel Wilson is anxious to get started. Do you have any questions of me or Colonel Wilson?"

"How long will it take to get to the Hudson River or Lake Champlain?" the Indian lady asked.

Levi answered. "There are so many variables that it's hard to estimate. It's about a hundred and seventy miles to either the Hudson or Champlain. My best estimate is one to two weeks. That will place us at either point of destination in the middle of November with winter coming on in an area of heavy snowfall. If you are unprepared for the reality on the ground, you should not make the trip. I'm not trying to scare you, but facts are facts."

"Colonel Wilson has vast experience in these matters, so take a few minutes to discuss the situation among yourselves, and let us know your decision," Colonel Howe suggested.

"I have one more statement to make. My small detachment is going to make the trip regardless of your decision. We have another hundred miles further to go before we arrive home. Time is precious, so think it over, lady."

She turned to face her band with a determined look and a firm set to her jaw. She asked them to make a vote. It triggered an eager response — all agreed to make the trip. Colonel Howe ordered a squad of soldiers to outfit the expedition.

Two hours later, the small convoy with the women and children in the two wagons and the male Indians mounted on horseback left the gate of the fort and took an easterly track over well-traveled paths bordering Lake Ontario. Two outriders on the flanks, a rear guard and an advance scout acted as guides and security protection to the convoy. For the first day, Levi wanted to stay close to the wagons driven by the women to see how they performed. The four men rode in a bunch close to the two wagons. He noticed that some of the men did not have very much experience riding horses. Thankfully, they were on gentle and stable mares.

The advance scout was setting the pace for the rest of the convoy. Levi had ordered him to maintain a speed that could be met by all of the animals without unreasonable delays to rest them. Levi liked to travel at a steady rate all during the day, so those who wanted to eat something midday should provide themselves with nourishment from dried venison or pemmican or whatever they chose.

Towards the end of the first day, Levi was able to detect a sense of achievement from the party, especially from the women on the wagons. He praised them for their trail discipline and skill in handling the two wagons over some very rough terrain. Some of the children elected to walk beside the wagons. It helped to burn off some of their excess energy.

Levi tried to engage the men on horseback in conversation and discovered that all of them had some ability to understand and to talk English. One of the youngest males, fifteen or eighteen years, told him that most of the people had been studying English. The lady in charge had been their teacher. He also found that her name was Aurora, and that her husband and son had died from disease, probably smallpox.

The advance scout was given the responsibility of selecting the overnight camping area, taking into consideration feed, water, and shelter for the horses and a suitable location for defense if that became necessary.

That first night, Levi estimated that they had traveled about twenty miles from the fort, good news considering they had gotten a late start. He ordered the two wagons to park side by side so that a canvas could be stretched between them to shelter those who did not sleep in the wagons. He did not want to assume command of their every move, and he was pleased to note that as soon as they halted, foragers rushed to gather wood for the evening fires. It was obvious that they were experienced forest travelers. The most valuable resource the convoy possessed were the horses, and their care was paramount in Levi's mind. He used an experienced eye to evaluate each of the mounts Colonel Howe had provided, and was not disappointed.

One of the wagons was full of grain and fodder. Their first stop provided excellent grazing and plenty of water. Since there were four adult males in the party, Levi requested that they join

119

his border scouts every two hours for picket duty on both flanks, front, and rear.

That first night after Angus had posted the picket stations Levi led his faithful Narragansett to the small brook to drink and to wet her hooves. He noticed that other horses were being given the same treatment. The lady called Aurora was close by with her sturdy Belgian horse that pulled the heavily loaded grain wagon.

"How did the Belgian work on the trail?" he asked.

It was dark beneath the heavy canopy, and she was unsure who spoke to her until she came closer. "Oh, this is a fine animal. The commandant gave us the best he had."

"I have a suggestion to make. We are going to be together for a while, so why don't we call each other by our proper names? I'm Levi Wilson, and one of your men told me that you are called, Aurora, a very pretty name."

"I think it will be easier, too. I have a confession to make. When we first landed at Fort Niagara, we were told that you intended to travel east. All night I thought about you, hoping that we could accompany you. Somewhere in my past, I had heard of you, and now I realize that I've known about you for a long, long time, Colonel Wilson."

"Levi, please, Aurora."

"If you wish, Levi. Do you remember a long time ago when you cared for and befriended a very young Penacook Indian whom you called Jo-Jo."

Levi was shocked. He had not thought about the incident in years. "I remember it well. He was a fine young man who could have had me killed, but he did not."

"He died several years ago from smallpox. He was my husband."

Chapter Fourteen

"Oh, my Lord," Levi exclaimed, shaking his head. "I remember Jo-Jo well. What a coincidence. We met when the frontier was alive with treachery, and I was very young. Now that I'm older, not much has changed except the large numbers of combatants. The strong always defeat the weak."

She studied his answer and asked, "Would you say that the British colonies were the stronger of the two combatants, or do you think that God was on your side? After all, England is one of the most powerful nations in the world."

Her logic was strong and direct, and he was slightly uncomfortable with the conversation. "I believe we had God on our team, because He gave us the right to live free. The desire to govern ourselves is a just concept because it elevates man's ability to accept his responsibilities. I believe God empowered our struggle for freedom. The Declaration of Independence is a noble document. I've spent my life defending the rights it defines, and I have conducted my life to be worthy of it."

"You have a nice way of putting it, Levi. Did it ever occur to you that the confederation of several of the Indian tribes in the east function under a similar system as you just described?" Aurora casually asked.

He chuckled to himself and replied, "Remind me to never debate with you, lady. I'm not well educated, I'm just a simple man of the forest, but I understand what you are saying. I have seen the full range of virtues and values which define the native peoples of this region. I like what I've seen with the Abenaki during our struggle with England. If I was an Indian, I would fight for my land the same way. But remember, the Indians fought each other just as fiercely as the white man fought each other. Like I said, the strong always dominate the weak."

"And now that you have a chance to build a new nation on the foundation of your noble principles, what do you think should be done about the native population that welcomed you to these shores? Shouldn't they have a voice at the council fires?"

"Dear lady, I'm just a simple soldier who tried to do his duty as God gave me the ability and the right to do so. Your questions are beyond my rank to answer. If I had a voice in such matters, I believe it would be just to give them a place at the council. I would grant them that, and I think they would give an honorable account of themselves. Now, if you'll excuse me, Aurora, I'm tired, and I want to rub down my faithful Narragansett for the night. He has earned it."

"I have been bold, Levi, and I ask your forgiveness. It was not my intent to place blame on you or anyone else. Sometimes I assume too much, but this evening, you have proven to me to be the honorable man my dear husband described years ago. I am comforted with that knowledge."

Later that evening, when everyone had settled down into their robes and blankets for the night, Levi and Angus sat quietly watching the burning coals of the campfire. It was a favorite time for reflection and review of the day's events. The friendly flickering of a campfire brought back memories of friends now gone. One of Levi's best friends had been Angus Campbell. Young Lieutenant Angus Campbell had proven to be much like his father.

"Are you anxious to put a roof over your head for the winter, Angus?"

"Yes, Sir. This is my last trail. I'm ready to take on the job of running the farm and sawmill at home. Lately, I've been thinking of a way that I could hook up a gristmill to be powered from the same sluiceway I use for the sawmill," young Angus replied.

"I'm ready to retire to the farm, too. These old bones have slept on wet and cold ground too many times. I hope you're right about this being our last trail, Angus. In time, we'll look back on our wanderings with nostalgic thoughts, remembering it as more enjoyable than it really was. I'll miss the friendship of many fine men who have gone on. I hope the country proves worthy of their sacrifice."

"I fear we're in for a disappointment, but we can hope." Angus stood up and placed a hand on Levi's shoulder. "I want you to know that it has been a pleasure to serve with you, Colonel. More than any man alive, you have developed a standard of excellence maintaining the virtues of men like my father. I'm sure that his spirit is here in the wilderness with us even now. If he could talk, I think he would say 'well-done.' Goodnight, Sir. I'll post the pickets tonight. You rest well, Sir."

"Thank you, Angus," Levi had replied in a low voice. Then, he left the fireside and settled down outside of the circle of light from the campfire, bundling in his bear robe and blanket. Sleep came easy when a man was exhausted.

In the middle of the night, Levi awoke to the sound of foxes yipping in the distance. A few minutes before, he had been dreaming about an incident he frequently turned to that never failed to gladden his heart and bring on a deep sense of loss and loneliness. It had taken place shortly before Beth died and Levi was outfitting himself for another long patrol of the upper Coos region. Beth had taken a small piece of fine linen and embroidered on it a small verse written by an English soldier during the bloody English civil war, and placed it in his coat pocket. He did not find it until two days later when he was deep within the frontier. It was a typical gesture of his gentle and lovely Beth, and it had touched his heart. He recalled the verse that night: "Oh Lord, thou knowest how busy I must be today. If I forget Thee; do not forget me."

The simple words of faith always comforted him. Just to remember the kind and considerate act brought a tremor to his lips. They had only three years together as man and wife. Now, after twenty odd years, she still held an honored place in his heart, and her memory was still strong and vibrant.

He was just dozing off to sleep when someone tripped over him and began to cry. Instinctively grabbing his loaded pistol under the bear robe ready to defend himself, Levi threw off the robe. In the limited light from the fire he saw that it was a child. He unlocked the pistol and placed it in his belt.

"What's the matter, Son?" He recognized James lying on the ground, afraid and crying. "Come now, James, are you all right?"

"I had to relieve myself in the forest and got turned around," he replied in a wavering voice.

123

"Don't be frightened. Does your grandmother know that you're here?"

"No, she's still asleep. I was quiet when I got up from the wagon. Now, I'm not sure which wagon it was..."

"Well, I have plenty of room under this bearskin for the two of us if you want to stay here with me the rest of the night. There are several more hours before dawn."

"Okay," he answered, crawling beneath the warm robe.

"You don't snore, do you?" Levi added, smiling at him.

"No, but some of them do over by the wagons."

"I'm sure they do. Well, you try to sleep and don't be afraid."

"Okay."

The weather in late October can be cold, especially first thing in the morning. Levi had been awake for some time hoping for a warm sunny day. An orange haze glowed in the eastern sky, granting his wish. James was sound asleep with his head laying on Levi's arm. Out of the corner of his eye in the limited light he spotted Aurora searching the wagons for her grandson. He waved his right arm to get her attention. She saw him, and walked quietly past the campfire toward him. He placed a finger over his lips and pointed to James who was still asleep. She saw him and the worried lines on her face instantly disappeared. A smile took their place. She nodded her head in approval and returned to the wagons.

Twenty minutes later, Levi carefully extracted his arm from James' head and crawled out from the snug cocoon. He watched the small boy for several seconds, and a warm feeling flowed through him. His Beth had once acknowledged how he had so completely accepted little Naomi, and told him that to be loved by a small child was a gift from Heaven. He was inclined to agree with her. This young and innocent child had come out of the wilderness to strange places and strange people, yet, he had felt secure in the powerful arms of this stranger. Levi felt privileged for the gift of trust.

The campsite was soon bustling with activity. Fires were crackling and tea was being brewed to ward off the brisk air of the autumn morning. Levi watched the women folding blankets and robes in preparation of another day on the trail to the East. Those men not on picket duty collected the horses and hitched them to the wagons. He had ordered that the saddles remain on the horses for added warmth during the night, and in case of an emergency they could be mounted in a hurry.

Aurora went to Levi's robe and gently woke James. He circled his arms around her neck. "I was worried about you, James, when I did not see you in the wagon."

"I tripped over Colonel Wilson in the night, and he said it was okay to stay with him. His bear skin was warm. I'm hungry, Grandmother."

"I'm sure you are. Come, we can eat and get ready to leave. Are you warm enough or do you want to be wrapped up in a blanket?" she asked him.

"I'm cold. The fire will feel good." Aurora placed a blanket around his shoulders and led him toward the campfire.

Eating on the trail or in the wilderness was serious business and was usually done in silence. After most had finished their hot tea, oatmeal, and smoked venison, Levi stood up to address the group.

"All of you have done very well so far on our journey. Your experience as wilderness travelers is evident, and I congratulate all of you. Now, I don't want to needlessly rush you, but we have a long distance to go. As I told you earlier, we will not stop for a midday meal. My goal is to reach the Genesee River by the end of the day. We'll cross it and camp on the eastern shore. We'll pause to supplement our food stocks with fish. Lieutenant Campbell has already stationed our outriders. If anyone needs any help, just ask. Are there any questions?"

A tall, muscular, young Indian raised his hand and asked in broken English, "What do we do if we are attacked by outlaws? We have no weapons other than our knives. I'm called Thomas."

"That's a good question, Thomas. If we are confronted with some of the scum that is present on the frontier, do not forget that our primary duty is to protect the women and children. If we are ever attacked, the second wagon should quickly pull beside the first one and stop. Women and children should seek cover within the wagons, not on the ground. That is important.

"Now, Thomas, you and your mounted friends should converge around the wagons, and my men will do the same. We do not have extra weapons, so you will have to depend on us to secure the outer perimeter. To be honest, I do not expect any unfriendly individuals will be able to penetrate our outer ring. Any questions?"

Aurora stepped forward to say, "We will do as you have requested, Colonel Wilson, and thank you for your concern."

"You are welcome, lady. Now let's complete breakfast and get this convoy moving."

The caravan continued to travel easterly along the shore of Lake Ontario until they came to the Genesee River, which they crossed at a convenient fording place and established a campsite close to the banks of the river. Salmon, trout, and whitefish were plentiful in the cold waters. The travelers were anxious to supplement their food supply.

They ate fish until they were full and moved on the next day with enough food for several days travel. Levi and his contingent had scouted the area and knew it well. They traveled around the southern shore of Lake Oneida with the intention of reaching Fort Stanwix on the Mohawk River. They were within sight of the fort five days after leaving the Genesee. The Fort would give them a chance to relax their guard and to obtain a few needed supplies from the fort's sutler store. It was a happy day when they rode through the gates of the fort. They had covered about a hundred and eighty miles. The two wagons needed some maintenance and the horses needed a well-earned rest. They had sustained no injuries, and not one of the group had been taken sick. It was a successful trek so far, and no one was more pleased than Levi. The balance of their trip to the Hudson River was spotted with several forts along the Mohawk River.

Fort Stanwix was built by General Philip Schuyler to protect the important portage between Lake Erie and the Mohawk River. Levi dismounted and walked into the Commandant's headquarters where he met a young Continental Army officer. "I am Colonel Levi Wilson of the New Hampshire Border Company, and I've just arrived at your fort with about twenty-five individuals. Over half of them are friendly Christian Indians. We request shelter and a chance to recuperate from several days on the trail."

"I'm Major Collins. I've heard of your Company, Colonel Wilson. We'll be honored to house you and your men, but the Indians, friendly or not, cannot reside in the fort. Those are the orders that I have been given and was told that there would be no exceptions."

"Major Collins, some of these Indians are women and children. We have an obligation to give them protection," Levi strongly stated.

"Orders are orders, Colonel. You know that," Major Collins replied firmly.

"I do, Major, but I also know that an officer has the obligation of disobeying an order that in his judgment is unjust and has the potential of creating more harm than good. If it helps, I'll personally vouch for and be responsible for their behavior."

The young Major held his ground. "I must repeat, Colonel, I will not allow any Indians to stay within the stockade of the fort overnight. They may use the fort's facilities during the daylight hours. At sundown, they must depart the stockade. I'm firm on that, Colonel. You and your men are welcome to stay as long as you wish."

"Thank you, Major," Levi replied, leaving the quarters. Lieutenant Campbell and the rest of the caravan were assembled in the middle of the parade field. He motioned for them to gather around. He repeated what the Major had told him and suggested that they leave the fort and establish a campsite nearby with pickets as they had always done.

Aurora stood up on one of the wagons. "Are you telling us that the officer in charge will not allow Indians inside the fort after sundown?"

"That is correct."

"Will he allow you and your men?" she asked.

"You are correct, Aurora. My men and I intend to vacate the fort with you. We made a promise to escort you safely to your destination, and we intend to keep our word."

They found a suitable site close to the Mohawk River in a stand of white pine trees. After foraging for firewood and tethering the horses in a green field near the bank of the river, with two hours before sundown, Aurora and two of her companions requested permission to enter the fort to purchase some tea. They had several fine fox furs to pay for the tea.

Levi confronted Aurora and her two friends. "I have no problem with it. The Major gave permission to do so as long as you're out by sundown which will be in another two hours.

That leaves you plenty of time. Stay together and check with me when you return. Lieutenant Campbell will accompany you to the fort's gate."

"Thank you, Colonel. I'm taking James with us."

An hour had passed, and Levi had not heard from the women. He called Angus who was bringing another armful of firewood to their campfire. Without warning, little James came running into the camp, frightened and crying. He told them that his grandmother and the other women were being held in the fort against their will by the soldiers.

"Grab your pistol, Angus, set the pickets for a tight perimeter, and follow me to the fort. James, you climb into one of the wagons and stay there until I return. Do you understand?"

He nodded his head as Levi and Angus took off at a dead run for the fort. They ran through the gate and found no one on guard. Something did not feel right to Levi. Shadows were beginning to gather as the sun approached the western horizon. He held out his hand to direct Angus against the stockade wall so that they could assess the situation. There was a light in the headquarters building and in the sutler's storehouse next to it. The enlisted men's barracks was dark which caught his attention. They stayed within the shadows of the wall and approached a window in the barracks. Suddenly the muffled cries of women could be heard from the barracks.

That was all that Levi needed to spring into action. He charged the door and smashed it inward with Angus behind him. There was enough light for them to see a woman on a blanket on the floor with several men taunting her. Levi leaped through the circle of men around the blanket knocking two of them down with his left fist. His right still held his pistol cocked and primed. Two men were trying to hold the figure down. It was Aurora. He grabbed the man closest to him and with one hand flung him against the wall, pointing the pistol at the man kneeling on the blanket. He stated in a clear voice, "Aurora, this is Levi. You there on the blanket, get up, or I'll kill you where you are."

The man looked surprised as Levi grasped him by the hair, lifting him off the floor. In one fluid motion Levi drove his knee into his groin with all his strength. The man howled in pain just as Levi smashed his head against his uplifted knee. Blood splattered all over his pant leg, and the soldier slid down to the floor, moaning in pain.

Angus had held the other soldiers at bay with his threatening pistol. "All right soldiers, this pistol has a hair trigger and is double loaded so that it will tear a big hole. Back off, now."

Aurora was still lying on the blanket on the floor. Her doeskin hunting frock was torn, and her pants were partly ripped open. Levi kneeled down and covered her with the blanket. "I'm so sorry that this happened, Aurora. Where are the other two women?"

Just then, Angus fired his pistol at one of the men who jumped him with a knife in his hand. The powerful charge picked him off the floor, smashing him against the wall where he collapsed, lifeless. Smoke from the discharge filled the room. "I warned you guys. The Colonel has another shot, so you can take your chances, or do as we tell you. Now, spread eagle on the floor."

Levi covered the men and kneeled closer to hear what Aurora was saying. "Ciera and Holly are in the next room. They hurt me dragging me across the parade ground..."

She was interrupted when Major Collins burst into the room with pistol in hand. "What in hell is going on here?"

"Major, you damn well better lead the way into the next room, or I'll do it for you." Levi threatened.

The major was quick on his feet and broke open the door to find that one of the women had already been partially undressed, and the other one trying to console her.

"I can't believe this outrage," Major Collins screamed at the two men in the room. "Corporal Harris, I want a full accounting of this incident now, or I'll step aside and let these border scouts do what they will to each of you, one at a time." He threw a blanket over the weeping lady on the cot.

Levi ran to the women. "Lieutenant Campbell and I are taking these three ladies back to our camp. I'll report to you later, Major. That bastard that's whimpering in the corner better hope that he never sees me again. He got off easy this time."

"I have a suggestion, Colonel Wilson," Major Collins quickly replied. "If the three ladies agree, they can stay overnight at the fort's infirmary where my wife may be able to help them. Food and hot tea is more readily available here than at your camp. You have my word that the three ladies will be well treated. You also have my word that the guilty individuals will be promptly punished. This fort was established to be a haven of security for those seeking safety. To think that three innocent women were attacked inside of this facility violates every standard of decency and justice expected of our new country and the Continental Army in which I proudly serve. That it happened on my watch leaves me with no option other than swift and harsh penalties. I profoundly apologize, dear ladies, and rest assured, you will be safe for as long as you stay with us."

Aurora heard what Major Collins said and spoke to Levi. "Perhaps it will be for the best if we stay here for the night. It will give us a chance to repair some of our torn clothing."

Levi was more than satisfied with the Major's response. Maybe he had been premature in judging him earlier. "I agree, Aurora. Major, your gracious offer of security and sustenance to the ladies is accepted. If you want me to prepare a statement of my actions, I'll do so before we leave."

"Your quick response to a serious breach of trust and faith has probably prevented it from accelerating out of control. This breakdown in order is intolerable. I thank you and Lieutenant Campbell. I would appreciate a report from you for the record. Now, let's get these three ladies out of here. Sergeant Blamey, place every man in this set of barracks under house arrest until further notice."

Chapter Fifteen

The rushing waters of the Mohawk River were the first things Levi heard upon waking at his usual time in the early hours of the morning. He had not slept well. The tragic attack against Aurora and her friends had troubled him all through the night. One soldier was dead and three innocent, defenseless women were violated by soldiers who had deteriorated to animals of the lowest order. The young major had handled the situation properly. Levi had no doubts that justice would be properly administered. He had shaken the major's hand when he and Angus had left the fort. If he was an example of the officers that were aspiring to join the new Continental Army, then Levi thought that there was hope for the new nation.

The major had told him that lawlessness was rampant on the frontier and had the potential of being even more destructive to the newly formed nation than outright combat between enemy formations. The threat came from within, and that made it more dangerous and difficult to resolve because the enemy was its own citizens! The place of the Native American who had welcomed the white man when he first reached their shores was far from reassuring. Differences in perception of land and land ownership was partially responsible. Terrorism was carried out by both sides, and a seething hatred of the parties competing for the land became well established. It was a stalemate that began to change when the British and the colonists battled for control of a continent.

The small group of natives with Aurora were caught up in the middle of the struggle for an empire. They were searching for their place in the sun and trying to adapt to the new rulers of the land. Throughout the war they had remained neutral even though their preference was that the colonists win the war.

131

Levi had seen it all from a very active position. In his own way, over the years, he had ridden endless trails in the wilderness and tried to dispense justice that was fair and appropriate. His early reputation as an Indian fighter eventually gave way to that of a champion of the Indians' many grievances. He firmly believed that the tribes had an absolute right to fish, hunt, and grow crops in their native lands such as the upper Coos region on the Connecticut River.

Levi was instrumental in arguing for the Abenakis' rights to both the British and the French, who wanted to build forts in the area. His passionate arguments to the New Hampshire Congress in Exeter were the main reason that Governor Benning Wentworth changed his mind about building a fort at the junction of the Ammonoosuc River and the upper Connecticut River. For generations it had been a focal point for hunting and fishing parties to meet and grow crops. It was the most important source of food production for several tribes in the New Hampshire Grants.

Levi had selected a position near the Mohawk River in a white pine stand to bed down. He loved to hear the wind sweeping through the canopies. It made a soft whirring sound that he found comforting and relaxing. The rush of water over a bed of rocks was like music to his ears. His beloved Beth had told him that without the rocks, the river would lose its song. The thought of her brought a smile to his lips. How fortunate he had been to have such a rich source of memories from the gentle lady. The short time they had been together was compensated by the richness of their relationship.

He was shaken from his reverie by the snap of a twig. Levi turned to see James slowly finding his way through the shadowy stand of pine. "I'm over here, James. Is anything wrong?"

"I was scared," James replied. "I'm worried about Grandmother."

Levi understood his concern. James was just a small child, yet he was troubled by the injustice that he witnessed. "Come here, James. You must be cold."

James was quick to crawl beneath the warm bear robe next to Levi. "Will my grandmother be all right?"

"Yes, you should not worry about her tonight, James. I believe she's in good hands. The major will see that she gets whatever help she needs. I thought it was for the best to leave her at the fort for the night. It's unfortunate that you had to witness the incident. It was uncalled for, and I'm certain that Major Collins will see that justice is done. Don't judge all white men by those creeps that attacked your grandmother and her friends."

"Why do they hate us?" he asked innocently.

"I don't have the answer to your question, James. After all of my years on the northeastern wilderness frontiers, I can't come up with any single reason for the bad feelings that exist in some people's hearts. Those who have been victimized by atrocities on both sides will probably always be bitter. Maybe it all boils down to what people think of themselves. Those who lack confidence or don't like themselves find pleasure in hating others they perceive to be inferior such as Indians or colored slaves. That fact gives them a dominant superior feeling in their twisted minds. You're too young to worry about those things, little man."

"I can tell when people don't like me just the way they look at me," James cried, laying his head against Levi's arm.

"Why don't you just close your eyes and rest easy until the dawn comes, okay?"

"Okay."

That next morning, a courier told Levi that Major Collins wanted to see him. Levi had no specific plans for the day except to prepare for the next leg of their journey home. He suggested to Angus that he organize hunting and fishing sorties for the men, and followed the soldier back to the fort.

"You must be an early riser, Colonel," Major Collins greeted him as soon as he entered the stockade.

"Old habits die hard, Major. How did your female guests make it through the evening?"

"They were magnificent. My wife volunteered to stay with them for the night at the infirmary. They spent half of the night repairing their torn clothing and drinking hot tea. They are strong, independent ladies who have weathered a traumatic experience with forgiveness and amazing grace."

"I had told you that they were Christians. It has been my experience that those natives who have converted to the faith and accepted Jesus Christ as their savior, practice their religion with more zeal than those of us who grew up in it," Levi said.

"I think you are correct, Colonel. My wife is still with them, so we won't disturb them right now. I really wanted to speak to you to ask a favor. I've spent most of the night investigating the serious breakdown in discipline. I've come up with four men who are responsible. They are now under arrest in my quarters, the only place secure enough to hold them."

"What can I do for you, Major?"

"If I supplied you with a wagon and two soldiers, a driver and a guard, would you accept the responsibility of escorting them to Albany where General Stark can better deal with their breaches of discipline? I'm anxious to remove them as soon as possible," the Major asked, watching Levi for his response.

"Before I answer that, Major, I'd like to ask the ladies if their presence will make them uncomfortable."

"I anticipated that reaction from you, Colonel Wilson. I've already asked the women, and they have no objections."

"Then you have your answer," Levi smiled. "General Stark will discipline the men. I'm one of his greatest admirers, and I also have the privilege of calling him a friend and a neighbor."

"He has an impossible task as commander of the Northern Department. General Washington has nothing in the way of funds or supplies that Stark requests on a daily basis. I served with him at Bennington. He was responsible for obtaining a commission for me. You and I did not see eye to eye when we first met, and I can tell you that General Stark was the one who gave me direct orders to allow no Indians in the fort at night unless they needed medical attention."

Levi nodded his head, "Well, I disagreed with your position, Major, but I understood the logic considering the violent history of the area. I'm going back to my camp to prepare for our trek eastward. We'll decide when to pull out after the women have settled in with us."

"I'll see to it that a sturdy wagon filled with supplies will be ready on a moment's notice. Thank you, Colonel. I've heard much about your border company. You live up to your reputation as a man of action. It has been a pleasure, Sir."

"Reputations are often overblown, Major, but thank you for the gracious professionalism. Our new Continental Army needs young officers like you, and I wish you good luck." Levi saluted the Major and walked out the gate.

134

An hour later, Levi was finishing an entry in his leather-bound log book, a habit he had continued for many years, when he heard loud shouts from the camp. Looking up he saw an army wagon with soldiers leading the three women into the camp. Anxious to get underway, Levi was pleased.

A short, heavy-set corporal jumped off the wagon and walked to Levi. "Colonel Wilson," he announced, "I'm Corporal Henry Baldwin. Sergeant Pat O'Malley and I have been selected to escort the prisoners with your wagon train. We have provisions for our use, and we'll gladly follow your orders."

"Welcome aboard, Corporal. I'd like you to take the rear position of the column behind our two wagons. I'll maintain flank and rear guard protection. Do you need any help with the prisoners?"

"No, Sir. They're scared to death of O'Malley. They've been trouble makers for a long time and have brought shame to our company. I was one of General Stark's militia recruits at Bennington. We have carbines and pistols with ample ammunition and powder on board the wagon. Major Collins gave us his personal pistols. He's a good officer."

"Henry, I'm glad to have you with us. Where are you and O'Malley from?"

Henry smiled proudly at Levi. "Both of us are from Rumford, New Hampshire, Sir. We've heard a lot about you and your border rangers. Say, that mount of yours looks like a Narragansett. They're the best I've ever ridden. My father raised several of them."

"We agree on that, Henry. My father raises them, too."

"I better get back to the wagon," Henry announced. "By the way, we have a few bushels of apples and several slabs of bacon we just took out of the smoke house. Your people are welcome to them. The apples came from a large orchard near the fort."

"Thank you for your thoughtfulness, Henry. Would you please distribute them among the Indians?"

He watched Henry return to the wagon and noticed a dark figure in a great coat rushing towards him. It was Aurora, wearing her hair loose about her shoulders. To his surprise she reached out to embrace him and kissed him lightly on the cheek. "Thank you for helping us. We were so frightened. The

135

mad dogs just leaped upon us without any warning. I prayed that you would come. Thank you."

Levi was unprepared for her embrace. "Dear Lady, I've felt guilty sending you alone." He released her and held her at arms length. "I hardly recognized you, Aurora, in that coat."

"The Major has been wonderful. He supplied each of us with these warm coats and boots that he took out of the fort's storehouse. I also want to thank you for taking such good care of James last night. He came to me earlier, and we ate breakfast together at the fort. We're ready to leave whenever you want."

There was a softness about her that touched him. It had been a long time since he held a pretty lady in his arms. "I was worried about you."

She tilted her head upward to look into his eyes. "You were not to blame for what took place. It is enough for me that you cared. I'm thankful for that."

He continued to hold her and replied in a strained voice, "How could one not care, dear Lady?"

She knew what he was trying to say and placed a finger to his lips. "We must not forget that shadows are fading on our lives and that we are of different races."

Suddenly, he was confused and searched for the right words when they were interrupted by Angus. "Excuse me, Colonel, but we're ready to leave."

Levi released Aurora who rushed back to her wagon. "Okay, Angus, get them in line," he ordered, turning to his mount.

The incident bothered him because, for a short moment, he completely lost control of his emotions. He had always prided himself with the discipline to keep emotions out of decisions. He had driven himself relentlessly ever since his Beth died. The minute Aurora placed herself in his arms, all the loneliness and heartaches of years on the trail had melted away from him as if by magic. He had the reputation of being a loner with nerves of steel. Such a posture was necessary for survival on the frontier.

Now, after all the years of devotion to the cause of liberty and freedom, he discovered in the middle of the vast frontier that duty to a noble cause was not enough. The soft touch of a woman had turned him inside out, leaving him confused and displeased with himself.

The wagon train left Fort Stanwix late in the morning on a well-worn cart track on the southern bank of the Mohawk River. They were making excellent time. Levi joined the advance scouts to make sure that they were alert for thieves and deserters from both sides of the war. They were more dangerous and brutal than the British or the rebellious Indians. He rode hard back to the wagon train and the rear guard, pushing the Narragansett to the limit. The cool wind across his face felt good.

Aurora was sitting beside one of the female drivers. He acknowledged her with a nod of his head. She smiled briefly and looked away. He hollered to them that he was pushing to make Fort Herkimer before nightfall where it would be safer for everyone. Minutes before sundown he led the column through the gates of the fort.

Levi, Angus, and Corporal Baldwin rushed to the headquarters building to plead for them to accept the women and children for the night. The captain in charge agreed to their request after Levi informed him of what took place at Stanwix. The two soldiers and their prisoners were also given quarters. The remainder of the caravan parked at a grassy glen next to the stockade and set up camp.

Angus organized the site with his usual efficiency. When that was taken care of, Levi suggested that the two of them escort the women and children into the fort for the night. The captain had told them that he would need a few minutes to secure adequate quarters for them. Aurora and the others were told about the arrangement. They collected those things they would need for the night and assembled for Levi and Angus. James was with Aurora when they approached.

Aurora spoke first. "Can James go with us women, Colonel Wilson?"

"If he wants to, Aurora, or he can stay with me. It's up to him."

"Are you sure he's not a nuisance?"

Levi frowned at the statement. "I'm not in the habit of saying things I don't mean. Like I said, the choice is his. He's a bright young man who deserves a chance for a future." Levi continued with a slightly unsteady voice. "I once had a small half-breed daughter that I loved with all my heart and soul. She died as an infant. Your grandson has touched that part of me that was buried with her. No, he's not a nuisance to me."

Aurora saw the sadness in his eyes and was concerned with that far-away stare his close friends frequently noticed and were so alarmed about. She reached and touched his arm. "Please forgive me. I didn't mean to stir up old memories. I know how painful they can be. Sometimes I think that I'm the only one to carry such a burden, and I know that is selfish. I had asked James, and he told me that he wants to stay with you. You should take that as a compliment, because he has been withdrawn ever since the death of his parents. He was especially close to his father who was a good man. I know that James is in good hands with you."

It was an emotional moment for him and all he could say was, "Thank you," and turned away from the wagon.

Angus witnessed the exchange. "Are you all right, Colonel?"

Levi looked at him with a stern stare, embarrassed that Angus had seen a part of him he had always kept to himself. "I'm fine, Angus. Come, let's help the ladies and the children into the fort. You can come too, James, to say goodnight to your grandmother."

Fort Herkimer had a much better set of interior structures than Stanwix. A small barracks building was set aside for the women and children with a secure guard detail positioned around it. It was obvious that the garrison was making every effort to welcome the weary travelers. Fish chowder, apple pies, and a large number of freely baked loaves of bread greeted the guests inside of the barracks facility. Levi and Angus smiled at the bountiful table.

James gave his grandmother a hug and told her he'd be good with Colonel Wilson. "Don't worry about me, Grandmother."

"I won't, my dearest James. Don't forget your prayers tonight. Goodnight. Rest well."

Levi saw the warm exchange between them. "Goodnight, Aurora. I wish you a pleasant evening."

She turned from James to Levi and said in a soft voice, "Thank you."

From that moment on, Levi and Aurora talked with each other often during the remainder of the four-day trip to Albany.

He was pleased to learn that they knew several people that each of them considered friends. One was Daniel Cullen, the publisher of the newspaper *COASTAL BEACON* from Portsmouth. Aurora had been a long-time student at the Memphremagog mission in Vermont where Lavina Cullen, a half-breed Ojibwa Indian known as "Whispering Wind" had worked years ago as a teacher, and as a friendly link between the Odanak community and the British government.

Now, the British influence was lost, and the Abenaki desperately wanted to make peace with the Colonial-American government. Their survival as a distinct race of people depended on their partial assimilation into the new world of the white man. Daniel and Levi had served together several times in the Hudson Valley-Lake Champlain region during the war with France. Lavina was known for her beauty and her compassion and commitment to the native tribes of northern New England.

Levi had told Aurora that the Cullens were a close family and they had lost their only son, Daniel III, who was an aide to Stark at Bennington. The fact that Levi and Aurora had mutual friends and acquaintances kindled a closer bond between them. She confided in him that it was her intention to return to the area so that James could be placed at the Charity School at Dartmouth in Hanover, New Hampshire. She had taught him to read and speak English, but he needed a formal education beyond what she was able to give him.

Four days after leaving Fort Herkimer, Levi called out to the weary travelers that Albany was in sight. He was anxious to visit with General John Stark, an old friend and neighbor. He even contemplated going down the Hudson River to New York City to catch a ride north on a merchant ship if heavy snows blanketed the area.

Chapter Sixteen

Several miles before arriving at General John Stark's headquarters at Stillwater, near Albany, Levi sent one of his men ahead of the train to inform them of their intention to stop and seek shelter for the night. It was getting late in the afternoon, and the drizzle had chilled everybody. The heavy snows that traditionally blanketed the area were not far off, and Levi was concerned for the Indian party, specifically Aurora and James.

A mile out from the Northern Department's Headquarters, they were met by a mounted escort sent by General Stark, led by a young captain in the Continental Army. He told Levi that they were welcome and to follow him. On the way, the captain explained that supplies and equipment were severely lacking, making Stark's job almost impossible. Several private homes, primarily abandoned Tory homes, were selected for the administrative needs of the Department. General Stark's son, Caleb, acted as his aide-de-camp. They stayed in a fine home on the bank of the Hudson.

The soldiers with the prisoners were diverted from the convoy to a different destination. Corporal Baldwin pulled abreast of Levi and hollered a farewell to him.

Levi waved, "Sergeant O'Malley and Corporal Baldwin, you've been worthy trail companions. Best of luck to you both."

The convoy was directed to a large barn that had been converted to barracks for soldiers that had fought the battle of Saratoga and had already gone south to Virginia. The barn was part of a large farm with acres of apple trees on the fertile soil of the flood plains from the Hudson and Mohawk Rivers. They drove their two wagons into the barn, giving them protection from the rain. Levi gave Angus orders to see that their charges were taken care of and immediately left to visit with his old friend, General John Stark. He crossed over the Hudson on a bridge and found the large white house which served as headquarters for the Northern Department.

John Stark was a modest man with deep-set eyes and bushy eyebrows. Smaller of stature compared to Levi, he was nevertheless a hardy and resourceful commander of men in combat. He was fifty-three years old. Many people found his serious demeanor and brusque ways intimidating, but those who knew him well remembered him as a warm compassionate human being. His pursuit of liberty and freedom for his country was rarely equaled, and his excellence in combat brought high praise from all who served with him.

The reunion of two veteran warriors was warm and heartfelt. John embraced Levi. "How good it is to see an old friend. I'm so glad that you survived this war, Levi. I always worried about you."

Levi was touched by the reception. His old friend had aged since they last met at the surrender ceremony of General Burgoyne at Saratoga. "You look good in that Brigadier General uniform. Is it John or General?"

Stark smiled, "I'll disown you if you don't call me, John like you always did. My arthritis has been giving me a hard time of late, but I don't complain. The war has been won, and this old war horse is ready to be turned out to pasture. I can't wait to return to my farm and dear Molly on the banks of the Merrimack."

"No one has earned that right any more than you, John. It looks as if I'm going to beat you home. This is my last trail. My wandering days are over. I've got some peach and apple trees that need my attention, and I'm going to enjoy staying in one place."

"Aye, we all dream of home and hearth," John said, remembering how it had been. "Once we've been reunited, and had a chance to look back upon our endeavors, we'll probably embellish them for our grandchildren, who will never know how it really was."

Levi saw a slight tremor on John's lips and understood. His dear friend felt the loss of every man who served with him, and would probably carry that sorrow to his grave. Levi grasped his friend around the shoulders and said: "The country is proud of your achievements, John. From the very beginning your dedication never faltered. You've been an inspiration to me all those years. I've always been proud to call you a friend and a neighbor."

That night, Levi and the rest of his men were treated to a festive evening with a supper of venison stew, chicken, and ham. General Stark offered them a sample of spruce beer, a specialty in the Northern Department. It was made from the new growth of spruce tree branches, molasses and spring water. It was a good source of vitamin C, preventing scurvy, an ugly disease causing loss of teeth and bleeding through the skin. Everyone thought it tasted terrible. Stark anticipated their reaction and told them that it was an old trick he had learned when he was an officer in Roger's Rangers many years ago. It was good that it tasted strong because it had a high alcohol content, and if not diligently rationed, the men could become unmanageable.

Levi and his men were a little over a hundred miles from home. There was no snow on the ground, so he made up his mind to make a dash overland instead of by boat, which could take another two weeks longer. Anxious to complete the journey, he left the comfortable home Stark used for his quarters and walked to the shelter where the other members of his train had been sheltered from the cold in a converted barn. Several fireplaces had been built in the converted stalls originally used by workers on the large farm.

Angus saw him enter the barn and rushed to greet him. "I hope you slept well, Colonel."

"The good general treated me like royalty," Levi replied, surveying the layout of the barn. "We stayed up late into the night discussing the state of affairs. The fight to gain our independence has exhausted everybody and has drained all of the meager resources the national treasury ever had. The issues that need to be confronted are daunting to say the least. John is ready to retire from service to his farm on the Merrimack, and so am I. Your generation, Angus, will have the task of making our republic work, and may the good Lord be with you."

Reflecting on what Levi told him, Angus replied, "That may be so, Colonel, but right now, all I want to do is return home as quickly as possible. I hope the folks have got enough firewood cut for the season; if not, my first job will be to harvest a stand of white ash near the house."

"That's known as the lazy farmer's brand of firewood," Levi smiled at his young assistant. "By the way, what have our passengers decided to do?"

"Most are returning to Odanak by way of Lake George and Lake Champlain and then north to the Saint Francis River. It's going to be a difficult trip, but they'll at least be in friendly country."

"Unless they run into criminal elements that abound out here in the frontier. They're like parasites that prey on the innocent ones unable to defend themselves."

"Well, Colonel," Angus began with a serious demeanor. "I've been thinking that maybe we could take them closer to their destination. I've talked to some of them. They would feel more secure if we accompanied them. What do you think, Sir?"

There had been a reluctance on Levi's part to abandon the party of Indians at this juncture, and he was glad that Angus had already made the decision easier for him. "I agree with your logic, Angus. Snows could come anytime. Perhaps General Stark knows of a supply train or some group making the trip north that could help them. He did not mention it to me, but it's worth asking."

"I understand that it's out of our way, Colonel. If you want to continue home without the diversion, God knows you deserve the right to make that decision, I would be willing to take the responsibility of delivering the party to the village encampment and then bring the men back home south through the mountains." Angus quickly laid out an alternate plan.

"I'm proud of you, Angus. You are truly your father's son. Let me ponder that for a while, and I'll give you an answer shortly."

Angus pointed to a door on their left. "The one they call Aurora and her grandson, James, are in this compartment, Sir."

Levi gave Angus a knowing glance. "I understood her to say that she was going to Hanover with the child." He avoided Angus's perceptive eye and knocked on the door. "It's me, Colonel Wilson."

Angus excused himself to check on the horses.

James opened the door. "Grandmother was just wondering what was going to happen. Good morning, Colonel."

143

"Good morning, James. How did you sleep?"

He grasped Levi's hand and pulled him into the room. The only light came from a small fireplace in the corner of the room. "I just placed some logs on the fire," James proclaimed proudly.

"You did well, James. Is your grandmother here?"

"I'm behind the curtain, dressing, Colonel. I'll be out soon. We slept well here in this comfortable room. How was your visit with General Stark?"

"Oh, we reminisced for hours. It was good to remember where we've been. I just spoke to Angus. Have you decided on your destination? Is it Odanak with the others, or do you want to go directly to Hanover?"

Aurora pulled the curtain to one side and confronted Levi. She was dressed in her traditional doeskin frock and pants, and seemed unsure of her answer. "It will probably be for the best if I stay with the other members."

"Angus agreed to accompany you to Odanak."

"How safe is the area from here to the village encampment?"

"General Stark told me that it's safer than the area we just passed through, but there are scattered elements of common criminals and deserters from both sides that can cause much harm to those unprepared to defend themselves. I'm concerned for the welfare of you and James and will certainly not abandon you until you are safe at the destination of your choice. You just told me what you should do; now tell me what you really want to do, please."

She looked into his eyes in the limited light of the fire and asked with a hesitation. "What do you think I should do, Levi?"

"I can take you directly to Hanover on horseback in three or four days. There are several good roadways from here to the Connecticut River. Like I said, Angus has volunteered to take your friends to Odanak. This is an alternative for you and James."

She grasped her hands over his. "Your proposal sounds wonderful to me, but I don't want to be a nuisance to you, Levi."

"Seeing you and James safely settled at the Charity School is hardly a bother. Friends help friends, you know."

She embraced him with tears in her eyes. "Thank you, dear friend. Thank you... I'm concerned about the weather, and

144

James is getting impatient with this long trip. Yes, anytime you're ready, we'll be ready, too."

"Then it's settled," Levi embraced her, smelling the bayberry scent in her coal-black hair. "Be strong a little longer, gentle lady. Before you know it, we'll cross the Connecticut and step into New Hampshire. I was pleased that Angus and the men volunteered to go to Odanak."

"Isn't it still dangerous to travel alone?" she asked.

"I've been thinking about that. Can you ride a horse?"

"Of course I can," she answered, surprised that he should ask such a question.

"I'll pick up another horse for you at Stillwater. We'll plan to stop for the nights whenever possible at inns along the way. There are several well-traveled roadways between here and the Connecticut. Travelers are most susceptible when they're camped for the evening. While I'm settling affairs with Angus and the men, you and James gather your things and wait here for me. I'll return with a horse. James will ride with me. We'll keep stops at a minimum and maintain a speed the horses can handle without exhausting them. How does that sound?"

Aurora was excited that the final leg of their long journey was about to get underway. "Thank you for being so kind and thoughtful," she whispered in his ear and softly kissed him on the mouth.

He returned her kiss and released her. "I'll be back soon for the two of you. I'd like to make it to Fort Anne by nightfall. That's about thirty miles. I know a small inn near the old fort structure. It's been burned, but I know the area well, so don't worry."

Levi returned with a horse and reviewed some rules of the road for the trip, especially in case they were confronted by heavily armed criminal elements along the way. "Whenever the roadway is wide enough, I want you to ride close beside me, Aurora. We stop for nobody unless they are heavily armed and outnumber us. I have two pistols with me and can return at least two shots at attackers, even at gallop speed. My motto has always been to run away from trouble and to resist with all possible firepower. Can you handle a pistol?"

"Yes, I can shoot quite well," she replied with a defiant look.

145

He handed her one of the pistols he carried in two holsters in front of his saddle. "Let's hope you never have to use it, Lady. It's primed and ready. All you have to do is cock it and pull the trigger."

She took it and tucked it in her waistband beneath the greatcoat. There was a sober determination about her that gave Levi encouragement. They spent a few minutes talking and saying good-bye to the Indian party and the border company members. Finally, he picked up James, placing him astride his Narragansett behind him, and leaped into the saddle.

"Let's get out of here," Levi announced.

An hour later, the three of them were crossing the Hudson River bridge to the eastern shore where they turned north along its bank to Fort Edward. Aurora was riding a gentle black gelding that John Stark had selected from his corral of horses. He jokingly told Levi that it had the heart of a lamb and the soul of a tiger much like the Narragansett he was riding. General Stark was known for his personal collection of fine horses. Levi trusted his judgment completely. Levi had picked up three leather pouches of pemmican, one for each to eat as they desired while still maintaining a steady pace.

It was a sunny day with a white frost covering the bare ground. There was a threatening feel of winter in the air that motivated him to move as rapidly as prudence and sound judgment permitted. James had clung to him tightly for the first few miles until he became used to the sure-footed pace of the Narragansett, then he released his hold and steadied himself with one hand. James was a child of the forest and was impressed with the grandeur of some of the fine houses they passed. There were still several log homes sprinkled about, but the bulk of them in this area of New York along the Hudson River were constructed of lumber.

Rich and productive soils of the Hudson Valley produced vast numbers of fruit orchards such as apples, peaches, and plums. Most had already been harvested, but an occasional tree was still heavy with fruit, waiting to be picked by returning soldiers now that the war was over. Levi and General Stark were anxious to do the same thing when they arrived at their farms in New Hampshire, thankful that they survived the cycle of violence.

Aurora was quiet and in a reflective mood. Memories of the past echoed through her consciousness. They always made her sad and generated a deep sense of inadequacy. She pondered with uncertainty just where she belonged in this new world that had been altered by a vicious war, shattering dreams that had sustained her and her people for a long time. The future was an empty void where she was desperately trying to find her place and that of her beloved grandson, James. Most of her life she had straddled two civilizations. Now she did not know where she belonged, and the most agonizing element of all, she did not know what she wanted. The lack of direction bothered her more than anything else.

She saw how James was happy to be riding with Levi whom he looked up to with childish adoration. It was a good thing, she thought, for Levi was a responsible role model for the young man. The disturbing thoughts that filled her heart brought doubt, anxiety, and worry. She was beginning to be weary of the emotional struggle. Having fixed the Charity School as a destination had only slightly eased the emotional load she carried. What if there was no room for her or James, and they were outright rejected?

Levi noticed that she was quieter than usual. She was worried about something. Even James noted her withdrawal and asked, "What's wrong, Grandmother?"

She looked at him with a forced smile. "I'm all right, James. Don't worry about me."

Glad that James had broken her reverie, Levi pulled the two horses down to a halt and turned to Aurora. "If everything is all right, then why are you trying to hide the tears in your eyes?"

Chapter Seventeen

Aurora could not deny the tears she held in check and pushed her mount into a gallop in front of Levi. The cool air felt good against her face. Something was happening to her! All during the trip she had been filled with joy that the war had ended, and she could fulfill her responsibility to James for an education. Now, she was frightened and uncertain about the future, and most of all, she had crossed the line she had vowed to never let happen. She had fallen in love with a white stranger she had only known for a few days. That admission was tearing her apart.

Over the years, she had cautioned several young Indian maidens about the dangers and heartaches that were certain to be a part of any relationship beyond their own race. She had not heeded her own advice, and it made her angry and confused.

Levi's Narragansett labored to catch her horse. He came abreast of her and forcefully grabbed the reigns, pulling them to a stop. He was angry at her. "What in the world did you think you were doing? You could have injured the horse in a chuck hole or been thrown from the saddle. What's the matter?" He leaped from the saddle and pulled her to the ground.

There, on a lonely stretch of roadway, she began crying uncontrollably. Her actions scared James. He had never seen her like this. "Grandmother, what's wrong?" he exclaimed hysterically.

She reached out to embrace him. "Don't be frightened, James. I've just been thinking too negatively lately that this thing we are doing just may not be the best thing for you."

Levi secured the two horses, listening to what passed between them.

148

"But we've talked a lot about the school, and we both agreed that it was time for me to continue my education beyond what Reverend Blyth could do at the mission. Why are you questioning it now?" James pleaded for clarification.

"James makes sense, Aurora," Levi hinted at what might be bothering her. "Are you afraid of being alone with me?" Her actions had planted seeds of distrust in his mind.

She quickly turned to dispel what he was thinking. "My emotional outburst is the result of many things I thought I had under control, Levi. No, I am not afraid to be with you. I apologize for upsetting both of you. Forgive me. Come, let's continue on our way. The horses will get a chill."

Levi shook his head. "Okay, if that's the way you want it. Whatever those bad thoughts are that made you so irrational will have to be resolved at some time."

"Yes, Levi, you're correct. Someday I shall..."

They rode in silence until they came to Fort Edward. Levi told them that he had been with General Stark when he captured the fort and placed an artillery battery on the other side of the Hudson. The act had effectively blocked Burgoyne's retreat from the battle of Saratoga to Fort Ticonderoga. It had been a brilliant tactical move by Stark, insuring the defeat of the large British army.

Aurora had gained control of her senses and surveyed the surrounding area with interest. Fort Edward had been the scene of a murdered and scalped white woman named Jane McCrea. The dastardly deed had gained wide circulation, generating a resentment for the excesses of the Indians that fought with both sides. Aurora explained to Levi that she had spoken to the Wyandot Indian maiden who had found the scalped body of Jane McCrea, the betrothed of a British officer serving with General Burgoyne's army who had sent the Wyandots to bring her safely to his quarters away from Fort Edward.

"The death of the lady caused quite a stir throughout the land. Burgoyne, to his credit, was outraged by the atrocity," Levi added to her story. "By the way, the mystery surrounding her death is the subject of much speculation."

Aurora nodded in agreement. "According to the Wyandot, Jane was hit by friendly fire from a detachment of Continental soldiers from Fort Edward that had come to rescue her. The

Hurons scalped her after she was shot. At least that's the story I heard. What a tragedy!"

"You know, Aurora, if we want to make it to the inn at Fort Anne, we should be moving on. It's about another twelve miles." Levi was pleased to see that she was alert and in control of herself. He helped her into the saddle and turned to James. "Are you getting tired, young man?"

James accepted his hand to climb on the Narragansett. "I am tired, but it has been exciting."

Two hours later, they arrived at a large inn near Oyster Creek on a well-traveled roadway between Albany and Rutland and the Connecticut River. Levi had used the inn several times in years past. The owner recognized him and stated that he did not normally allow Indians to use his inn, but since the woman and child were with him he would make an exception.

Levi had placed several gold coins on the counter which influenced the exception. Two rooms were made available — one for Aurora and one for James and Levi. The first thing Levi ordered was a warm bath for the three of them. The owner told him that they had plenty of hot water available for their needs.

James and Levi took their baths in the woodshed of the inn. The large wooden tub was placed next to a fireplace where the inn cooked their meats in a spit attached to a crank which turned the meats over the flames. Levi made sure that James soaped himself all over, then rinsed him with a pail of warm water. They laughed a lot, scrubbing off the accumulated dirt and grime. It felt invigorating to change into fresh clean clothes, displacing the aches and pains of the day's ride like magic. Now they were hungry!

Aurora had completed her bath in her room and waited for James and Levi to come after her. She thought it was prudent to not appear in the tavern room alone. She had dressed in a clean doeskin dress with intricate designs of beads woven onto the soft hide and had combed out her hair, letting it fall about her shoulders. It still smelled from the bayberry soap she had used. Levi announced himself and gently knocked on the door.

He saw a different Aurora open it. "This is the first time I've seen you without your hair in braids. Are you as hungry as James and me?"

"I believe so," she smiled. "The bath felt good. Thank you for suggesting it."

They took seats at a table in the tavern room near the large fireplace with long strands of fire reaching up into the flue. The heat was welcome. A loaf of warm bread was placed on the table. Levi ordered hot beef stew, strong cheddar cheese, and apple pie. They were relieved to have a change of diet. Aurora nodded her approval of his selections. The owner brought Levi a hot mug of coffee, an item available to communities accessible to shipping from the Caribbean. Levi sipped it cautiously and ordered honey or maple syrup to sweeten it. He also ordered cold milk for James and Aurora if they would like some.

Aurora was quick to reply. "Cold milk would be a real treat for both of us."

"We have plenty," the owner admitted, turning toward her. "You speak English better than any native I've ever known."

She smiled at the owner who meant it as a compliment. "Thank you. Now that the war is over, those of us who live in this country should be able to communicate with each other."

The owner returned her smile. "That makes a lot of sense, Lady. I'll get you two mugs of fresh milk."

Levi was proud of her response. "You handled that with grace, Aurora. The way you have your hair is becoming to you."

She blushed and looked down at her bowl of beef stew. "I'm not used to compliments, but thank you just the same. You are a very generous man, Colonel Wilson. I did not expect you to pay for lodging and food."

The hint of independence made him wonder even more about just who this lady was. "A Christian should be charitable, and I'm glad to help. Tell me, Aurora, if you did not have James to care for, where would you be, and what would you be doing? It's not my intention to pry into another's affairs, so if you choose not to answer, I understand. Your response to the innkeeper impressed me that we all should work in harmony to make this new country function properly. You and your people have been forced to make many changes simply because a stronger force has imposed their will upon your way of life.

"Whether that is right or wrong, history will have to determine. What I'm trying to say is that I'm not an enemy of your people and never was. I've spent my life fighting the

151

enemies of justice. Wherever violence has erupted, I've tried to bring peace, hoping that the Lord was guiding my way. No one hates war as much as a tired old soldier. I hope that the peace we have won on the field of battle against our motherland will bring an acceptable level of justice to your people. I believe that some progress has already been made with you being welcomed at this inn."

She listened carefully to this sturdy frontiersman beside her, catching a glimpse at his inner soul. It brought a cloudy mist to her eyes. "Not everyone is as charitable as you, Levi. You ask me what I would be doing if I did not have James to worry about. Well, caring for him and seeing that he is better prepared for adulthood all falls within my dreams of being an agent for change between my people and your western society. I do not know exactly how I implement the dream, but it would be my goal. It was also the dream of my husband, Jo-Jo, as you called him, for the two societies to co-exist with tolerance and respect from both parties. More than anything else, I dream of peace and harmony, but I'm afraid it is not to be."

He reached across the table to grasp her two slender hands in his gnarled fingers. "Dear Lady, you have taken on a monumental task that will take a long time, but it has to start at some point with one person at a time. I've seen a different attitude with the St. Francis Indians during this war compared to their involvement in the war with France. Much progress has already been made."

"Several Abenaki bands have joined with the New Hampshire rangers to patrol and scout the northern frontiers between Canada and New England. Perhaps peace will prevail now that the actual fighting is over. Their desire was to remain neutral during the revolution, yet, a greater number were sympathetic to your cause against the British," Aurora said, taking a long drink of milk. "Mmm, it is good. It's been a long time since I had fresh milk."

The large fireplace in the tavern lit up the room with its flickering flames, creating shadows that fell across her face. She had struck a pensive pose, turning to watch the embers. She was a lady of endless moods. Levi perceived that a person could live a lifetime with her and still discover new things about her.

She turned from the fire and confronted him in a serious mood. "You ask me about the future. What about you, Levi? Is this the last trail for your border company?"

"My immediate answer is 'yes'. This has been my life for forty years. I'm almost fifty-five years old, and I yearn to remain in one place for the rest of my days, God willing." He sighed, and as an after-thought continued: "However, if there was a need for my services, I would not refuse as long as it contributed to the winning of the peace. That may be more difficult than any of us imagine."

"Don't you have any family waiting for you in New Boston?" she asked. "No… please disregard that question. I had no right to pry into your private world."

He smiled at her. "I asked you a question, and it's only fair that you have the same opportunity. My wife, Beth, and her half-breed daughter both died many years ago. The farm is being run by my cousin, who lives nearby. I hope to take it over when I arrive home."

"You deserve an interval of peace. The concept of home has a special meaning to those who have been away for a long time. What a gift it must be…"

"Where is your home, Aurora?" Levi asked, wondering what she would say.

She replied, "There is a wonderful English sentiment that home is where the heart is. My original home with the Delawares was in what you now call New York. I've traveled many times over most of the wilderness region east of the Ohio River, and can honestly say that my longest stay has been at the mission at Memphremagog. My husband, as you know, was a Penobscot. We lived for a time in what you now call Maine. For now, my home will be wherever James can get an education."

Young James had been listening with interest at the exchange between his grandmother and Levi. Even at his young age he understood what she was sacrificing for him. The large amount of food he had consumed, combined with the warmth of the fire, was making him drowsy.

Levi noted his condition and laid a hand on his shoulder. "Are you ready to go to bed, James? We have a busy day ahead of us tomorrow."

"I am sleepy, Colonel," he replied, getting up from the table.

153

"We'll meet you here in the morning, Aurora. Sleep well."

"You, too, Levi," she answered in a soft voice. "I am weary, and a soft bed will feel good."

The fireplace in the small room shared by James and Levi had warmed the room by the time they arrived to retire. Levi laid James down and covered him with woolen blankets. Minutes later, he was sound asleep. Levi sat in the large chair beside the fireplace and reviewed the last few days. His immediate thoughts were with his border company under the able leadership of Angus. He had been responsible for their welfare for so long he felt naked alone. They had filled his days. Being responsible for them and the pursuit of any mission assigned to them left little room in his life to think of himself or his own personal needs.

He had told Aurora that he was anxious to return home, and that was true, but going home to an empty house filled with memories of times long past left him with anxieties that surprised him. Was that what he really wanted? He could not answer the question with certainty.

The flames eventually died down. Levi banked the coals for the evening and went to bed, dreaming of the days of his childhood, especially those long winter periods where their home was an island in a sea of snow. Their home on the hilltop was buffeted with winds out of the west. Snow often swirled with great velocity around the farm buildings. Those had been happy times for him, when the family gravitated to the large fireplace in the kitchen. On severely cold nights, he curled up on the cot beside the fireplace so as to keep the fire going. He smiled at the vast amount of firewood required to keep the four fireplaces in the house functioning. Cutting wood was always a "work in progress." His father had been adamant about burning well-seasoned hardwood. He had called it "sizzle-free" and Levi had continued the tradition of seasoning the wood, especially red oak, for two years before burning.

Early the next morning, the three continued their trek into northern Vermont, an area most considered safe for travelers. James was still sleepy, so Levi had him ride in front of the saddle so that he could support him. He leaned back against Levi and fell asleep. Aurora and Levi smiled at his inability to stay awake. They traveled for several miles into the mountainous region of central Vermont.

Aurora wore her great coat with a scarf around her head. The day was cloudy with high winds that were cold unless one was well-protected. Even with her great coat she was chilled. They came to a section of the well-traveled track where a tree was blocking their advance. Levi instantly became alert for trouble. He saw two men off to the side with muskets in their hands. He knew then that it was a trap, and he was angry that he had been caught unaware. He reached out and grabbed Aurora's horse to a halt. They were far enough from the men that their smooth-bore muskets could not reach them with accuracy.

"Aurora, come close to take James from me. Hurry!"

She did as he sternly demanded. James climbed behind his grandmother and anxiously held her. "What are we going to do?" she exclaimed.

"You take James and ride back on the road several hundred feet and turn into the woods wherever you can find good cover. Wait until I return. If I'm not back within ten minutes, ride as fast as you can to the nearest cabin or house. Do you understand?"

"Yes, but..."

"No buts, Aurora. I can handle this, now move!"

She reluctantly did as she was ordered. Levi waited until she had left the sight of the two armed men and then turned the Narragansett into a hemlock stand close to the roadway where he had a perfect view of the road and the two men. He quickly yanked his carbine rifle from its scabbard and took a position against one of the large hemlocks, drawing a bead on one of the men.

"Ahoy, yonder," he called out in a strong, clear voice. "You with the muskets, I'm ordering you to drop your weapons and lay down on the ground. I give you three seconds to do as I say."

Both men raised their muskets and fired at the grove of hemlocks where they heard his voice. Their balls fell a hundred feet in front of Levi. He had hoped that he could settle the situation without violence. Since he was forced to defend himself against foes intent on killing him, he calmly held his sights on one of the men hurrying to reload his weapon, and squeezed the trigger. Levi had loaded his carbine with an extra heavy charge of powder. The bullet hit the man with such force it spun him around before he fell to the ground.

"Unless you want the same treatment," Levi cried out to the surviving man, "Do as I have told you. Throw your weapon away from you." He was vigorously loading and priming his carbine as he spoke.

The second man answered by firing again in Levi's direction. Without hesitation, Levi leveled the carbine and calmly returned fire. The man emitted a loud cry of pain and fell backwards. Levi took several seconds to reload his carbine before leaping into the saddle, urging the Narragansett to the scene of the dispute. On horseback, Levi much preferred to use his pistols and held one in his right hand as he approached the two downed men. He secured the horse to a white birch sapling and cautiously approached the bodies. The first man was dead with a large chest wound. The second man was beginning to stir, and Levi kneeled to check on his condition, turning him over on his back.

Without warning, the man hit him hard in the temple with a rock. It dazed him for a second and caused him to drop his pistol. The man had been hit on top of his right shoulder, and lurched for the pistol with his left arm just as Levi instinctively smashed him in the head with his fist. "One more move like that, and I'll kill you," Levi threatened. "Now, how many are there of you? Answer truthfully, or suffer the consequences."

The wounded man saw the look of determination on Levi's face and quickly confessed that there was another man further down the road around the bend. "Call for him to surrender, or you'll be the next victim."

The wounded man staggered to get to his feet when he cried in a shaking voice what had taken place. Levi stood off to one side, watching his captive carefully and at the same time, keeping an eye on the roadway around the bend. Two more men walking towards their location soon entered his line of sight. Levi, a little concerned that he now had three men to deal with, grabbed the coil of rope he always had attached to his saddle and firmly fastened the wounded man to a tree nearby.

As soon as the other two heavily bearded, roughly kept individuals came closer, he ordered them to place their hands behind their backs where he tied the free end of his rope around their hands, leaving enough rope to tie the men to another tree.

Wondering what he was going to do with them, he called in a piercing voice for Aurora to come to him.

She answered in a shrill tone that she was on her way. James was all eyes when the dead man's body came into view. Aurora saw it and winced, concerned about Levi's safety. She climbed down from the saddle and pulled the pistol from beneath her great coat, turning it towards the helpless prisoners. "Are you all right, Levi?"

"Yes," he replied, checking the tightness of his rope.

One of the prisoners spit a large cud of tobacco at Aurora, landing on her coat sleeve, and at the same time, kicked her in the stomach, bowling her over backwards.

Chapter Eighteen

Aurora cried out in pain at the sharp jab of the man's boot into her side. Levi ran to collect her in his arms. "The dirty coward. Are you seriously hurt?"

"No, he just surprised me. I should not have gotten that close to him. I'm all right, Levi." She looked into his cold eyes.

Levi released her and ran to drive his knee into the man's groin with all his might. The man crumbled with a loud moan. "Try that again, and you'll die a slow and painful death," Levi threatened. "Don't I hear an apology to the lady?"

The man looked up from his slumped position with a sneer. "No Injun is a lady."

Levi instinctively smashed him in the face several times, and would have continued if she had not restrained him.

"No, stop it, Levi..." screamed Aurora. "He's not worth killing!"

Breathing heavily, Levi stepped back from the prisoner. He was thinking what should be done to the men when a train of four wagons appeared from the opposite direction and stopped at the downed tree still blocking the road. Levi hailed them and told them what had taken place.

The lead teamster got off his wagon seat to look at the men. He recognized one that had kicked Aurora. "I had a feeling about this guy. He was hanging around us checking what we had on board when we were back on the Connecticut."

"We probably upset his plans to steal your wagons," Levi surmised. "What do you have in the wagons?"

"Foodstuff mostly with some blankets and gunpowder headed for Fort Edward," the burly teamster replied.

"Will you take the prisoners off our hands? I'm Colonel Wilson of the New Hampshire militia. General Stark is a good friend. If you tell him what happened, he'll see that justice is done. We're headed for the Connecticut and are anxious to be on our way."

"Sure, we'll be glad to turn them over to the detachment at the fort. You were lucky. There are a number of robber bands, and some of them are ruthless killers," The teamster chuckled. "It looks as if this bunch picked on the wrong party."

"I'll help you remove the tree," Levi offered, shaking the teamster's hand.

"We can handle it. I was ready to take a small break anyway."

"I'm much obliged to you," Levi answered, lifting James onto the Narragansett. "Are you able to continue, Aurora?"

She shook her head and mounted. Levi could tell that she was hurting. "I'll be all right."

Five minutes after they left the bend in the road they heard three shots in rapid succession. Levi turned around to check on the shots. He looked at Aurora with a stern tilt to his jaw. "Let it be, Levi. With the absence of civilized law and order, man does what he must to survive. Sometimes it's cruel and unjust, but when it is the only form of restitution available, it's probably better than no consequences for predatory acts."

Her response to the assumed act surprised him. He remained quiet for several miles. They had entered the mountainous region of central Vermont which could place an added strain on the horses, dictating more rest stops at areas with good grass and water. So far, their luck had held, and no snow hindered their progress. Levi suggested a stop at midday to rest the horses. He selected a spot with adequate feed and a small trickle of a stream. Each of them had not eaten anything since leaving the inn, and they were hungry.

Levi grinned to himself as he lifted James from the Narragansett. "I have a surprise change of diet from the soggy pemmican we usually eat. Early this morning I had the innkeeper put up a lunch for us consisting of chicken, cheddar cheese and a fresh loaf of bread. He also threw in several fresh apples to munch on."

His surprise pleased Aurora and James. "That will taste good, Levi. Thank you for your thoughtfulness."

Levi refilled their water canteens in the stream and passed them around. "The bread is a heavy molasses bread that needs some water to help wash it down," he chuckled to himself, pleased with his surprise.

"You're going to spoil us on this trip, Levi," Aurora replied, sitting with her back against a white ash tree. She had been thinking about what was ahead for them.

Levi anticipated her pensive pose. "When was the last time you were at the Charity School?"

"About a year ago," she answered. "It was the first time I met a marvelous Negroid lady by the name of Rose Waters. She was working as an assistant to the officials of the school and as an all-around advisor to the students. She told me when I left that there would always be a place for me at the school. I'm hoping that the same offer is still available along with an enrollment of James into the school."

"And what if neither is available to you, Aurora? After all, a year is a long time, especially in these troubled times."

"If that is the case, then I'll return to the mission at Memphremagog. I'm certain that I can earn my keep there," she stated with confidence.

Levi finished a piece of bread and cheese, thinking about her answer. Her plans were tentative but obtainable, with some luck. "I remember talking to Daniel Cullen one day right after the battle at Bennington. His only son, Daniel III, was killed. He and his wife, Lavina, were like lost souls for a long time. The Rose Waters you mentioned was engaged to their son. I couldn't recall her name until you mentioned it."

"Over the years, I've met Lavina several times. She was a wonderful advocate for the native people and had worked tirelessly for their benefit. She's an Ojibwa."

"You're right," Levi remembered well. "They have one of the most remarkable marriages I've ever witnessed. Their work with the COASTAL BEACON is widely recognized as one of the most respected newspapers in the colonies. I'm proud to call them my friends. Dan was one of my border rangers for a short time after the war with France ended. He was a seasoned veteran with a distinct hatred for the Abenaki, who killed his first wife and son. Of course, that changed over the years, but right after it took place, he was a ruthless foe to all Indians. His wife has softened that part of him."

Aurora listened with interest, for she had met both individuals and always enjoyed reading the editorials in their newspaper. Now, Daniel Cullen was a very vocal crusader for the rights of the native people. She was pleased to learn that Levi had similar convictions and harbored the same sentiments. She could imagine that Levi, in his quiet unassuming way, may have been an influence on his friend's change of attitude.

Later in the day, they came upon a small inn with only one room available. Levi had stayed there several times over the years. This portion of Vermont had been a stronghold for the Tories, but now their influence had waned, and most accepted the change that had been won on the field of battle. Only one room was available, and Levi insisted that Aurora take it. He and James could sleep in the barn filled to capacity with sweet smelling hay. That evening passed uneventfully, and the new day dawned with a bright sun rising in the eastern sky. It was perfect weather for the final segment of their journey to Hanover.

The roadway was smoother and wider than any they had encountered earlier. They were entering that portion of the frontier that had converted from wilderness to rural farms. Levi felt an urgent desire to go home. This trip alone with Aurora had given him a chance to reflect on the future.

His transition from the terror of combat to this period of peace was unsettling to him. For years, he had always been mentally prepared for the uneventful appearance of violence and possible death. Without realizing it, he was held hostage to the responsibility for his men and the missions they had been assigned. It had created a form of pressure that he could not discard at will — it was always there.

The fact that he was no longer needed left him feeling empty and lost. It had been a way of life so demanding that he had completely dismissed the kind of plans and dreams that give meaning to the lives of most people, like his mother and father and cousins, who could never fathom exactly what he lived with for years without end. The commitment he had made early in life to the cause was something he never regretted, but sometimes he yearned to be free of the responsibility.

All during this trip back to his beloved New Hampshire, Levi had been thinking of little else. His enthusiasm for the peace and quiet of home was somewhat dismissed by a strange feeling of insignificance. The massive contrast of combat and the peaceful environs of home was difficult to accept. Every warrior experienced the same phenomenon. It was often bantered about by veterans of warfare, so he knew that it was not unique for him to be affected by the new way of life ahead.

The roadway from Woodstock gave them two options. They could travel north across the White River, then cross the Connecticut at Hanover, or they could continue in an easterly track across the Connecticut to Lebanon and then head north to Hanover. Levi decided to take the route to Lebanon where they only had to cross the Connecticut. It would be slightly longer but would be easier. He knew the area intimately.

Aurora was quieter than usual on this last day. Levi saw the apprehension and worry on the lines of her face. They had not been there when they first met at Fort Niagara. That seemed a long time ago, and he had come to respect and admire the mystical Aurora with the dark flashing eyes and the soft, melodious voice. He had watched her carry on day after day without complaint or a discouraging word. She was a lady committed to her mission of being responsible for James' welfare without a thought about what she wanted.

Now, near the end of their journey together, Levi was being visited by feelings he had not experienced for years. They contributed to the uncertainty and confusion that haunted him. He seemed to lack control of himself, and that bothered him more than anything else.

She was aware of Levi's study of her and lifted her eyes to meet his. She smiled with that hint of sadness that she tried to hide from the world. She was a lone crusader at a time when crusaders were unwelcome in a world exploding in change and upheaval. Some would have dismissed her intentions as out of touch with reality.

Levi wondered, watching the wind blow strands of black hair across her face, if she had prepared herself for the possibility that her dreams and hopes for the future were not shared by others. That potential for failure struck him deeply, for he had assumed responsibility for her. Failure could destroy her positive outlook and wash away the dreams which defined the lovely Indian lady.

That was the word that defined her — lady! She was more of a lady with her army great coat and gray scarf wrapped around her head than any of the grand ladies who moved within aristocratic and social circles with their expensive gowns and jewels. Sadly, he recalled, she would never, under any circumstances, be accepted as an equal...

The Connecticut River held so many memories for him that when it came into view he let out a hurray of a holler. He had considered the river as the point where the cruelties of the frontier were displaced by the benevolence of civilization. It was like entering into a new world where dreams could come true, and one could shed the ugly companion of dread and the uncertain potential for violence that might exist just around the bend of the trail.

"Oh, it's like coming home," he cried. "Many a day I wondered if I'd ever live to see this again."

Aurora witnessed the effect the river had on Levi. He was like a little boy. She shared his euphoria. "Arriving at a familiar place after a long absence and a long journey is truly a time of great joy and thanksgiving. I'm glad for you, Levi."

They took the ferry across to Lebanon. Levi nudged the faithful Narragansett off the barge up the bank of the river into New Hampshire. "I've crossed the river countless times in my lifetime, but never with the same sense of joy that I now feel. I'll remember this crossing as the most memorable in my life."

She followed him off the ferry barge, smiling at his outburst. "We've got about another ten miles to go."

Levi nodded his head in agreement. "There's a nice little tavern just up the roadway. Why don't we stop to have a meal that someone else cooks? We can relax and celebrate this important day for the two of you."

"Your generosity and kindness humble me, Levi Wilson. I do not have any money or possess anything of value to repay you..."

He pulled the Narragansett beside her and placed a finger to her lips. "Hush, Lady. I do this because I want to, and I am able to do it. This day is worthy of celebration, and besides, it will be a farewell toast to a successful endeavor that has been most pleasant on my part."

She grasped his hand and squeezed it. "You are a remarkable man. How can I refuse your thoughtful gesture?"

Throughout the meal of beef stew, thick with fresh potatoes and carrots, Aurora was displeased with her reluctance to enter into the festive spirit of the occasion. The unknown that awaited them at Hanover dominated her thoughts and feelings. Would the school take James? Would there be room for her to work at the school? Fear of the unknown was wearing her to a nervous state she found most uncomfortable. Levi told them several funny stories about his stops at this same tavern in past years. James laughed at them. Aurora smiled, but her heart was not laughing.

Levi recognized what was holding her back and quickly paid their bill when everyone was finished. They were finally on the last leg of their journey together. Recognizing that she was preoccupied with her own personal thoughts, he set a fast pace to eat up the miles as quickly as possible. That also helped to remove the unsettling thoughts from her immediate consciousness. An hour later, they first saw the spires of a church tower in the distance.

Dartmouth College had been commissioned by the state in 1770 by Governor John Wentworth, an Englishman who truly loved New Hampshire. The school was run by Eleazor Wheelock, a minister who opened the doors to English youth. He also formed the Charity School to provide Indian and Negro youth with an education. Now that the new nation had been formed, there was a chance that the youth of the period could lift the nation out of the ashes of civil war with their brethren across the sea.

The extent of the beautiful new buildings of the college awed Levi. He could remember when the area was dotted with rustic log cabins, and the inhabitants had feared for their lives when the Abenaki ruled the wilderness. Times had changed! Aurora was familiar with the layout of the buildings and led the way to the Charity School, a two-story wooden building with a high steeple on the roof. She pointed to a hitching post beside the structure and anxiously dismounted.

"I'll go inside," she said, removing the scarf around her head. "James, you stay with Colonel Wilson. I won't be long." With that, she opened the front door and disappeared.

Several minutes later, she reappeared, flushed with happiness and thanksgiving. A young Negro lady followed on her heels. "Levi, this is Miss Rose Waters. Rose, meet Colonel Levi Wilson, and my grandson, James."

Levi removed his green Glengarry cap. "I'm glad to finally meet you. I've heard much about you, Miss Waters. This young man here with me is James. He's ridden hundreds of miles without one complaint."

James extended a hand to Miss Waters who quickly brushed it to one side and embraced him warmly. "Young men like you are the main reason we have the school. Welcome, James." She turned to Levi and looked up into his eyes. "And I have heard much about you, Colonel. Our mutual friends, Daniel and Lavina Cullen, have spoken often about you. Thank you for bringing James and his grandmother safely to us. There is much to be done here at the school and we welcome Aurora with open arms. She's a very brave and dedicated champion of her people and of the power of an education to enlighten them so that they may take their proper place in our society."

Levi was impressed by the articulate, well-spoken Negro lady. She spoke from her heart, and he was pleased to learn that they had a place for Aurora at the school. Now, her dream of making a difference could become a reality. He was proud of her. Within a few minutes, the drawn lines that had framed her face had disappeared as if by magic. She glowed with excitement and joy.

Anxious to get on his way, Levi said good-bye. "Well, Aurora, this is where we part. I'm glad that things worked out for both you and James. I'll remember this trip with warm smiles and faithful companionship." He picked up James and embraced him. "This is not good-bye, James. I'll see you again. If you ever need anything, you tell Miss Waters. She'll get in touch with me, and I promise to be there for you. You've been a brave young man, and I will miss you."

"I'll miss you, too, Colonel Wilson," he replied with tears in his eyes.

Rose took James from Levi. "Come, James, I'll show you your new school. Bon voyage on your trip home, Colonel. Thank you for everything."

"Thank you, Rose Waters."

Thankful to be alone, Aurora began to empty the saddle bags on her horse. "No, Aurora. The horse is yours to keep. We can't take it back to Albany. I'm sure the kind General intended for you to keep it."

She nervously placed her few belongings against the hitching post and looked up at him. "How does a friend say thank you without shedding a tear? This parting is more difficult than I anticipated. You will always be in my prayers. Thank you for your generosity and your kindness, and thank you for the strong security blanket you had placed around James and me. I never was afraid for one moment on the trip. You have given me more than you think. James now has a chance for a new life, thanks to you."

"Oh, no, dear Lady. Thanks goes to his courageous and lovely grandmother. Guiding you to this place has been a privilege, Aurora. When we started it, I did not know what to expect. Now, the trail will be lonely without your presence." She saw what was in his heart and moved softly into his outstretched arms. They kissed and embraced, not wanting this moment of discovery to pass.

He found his voice first, and asked in a strained tone, "Promise me that if you ever need anything, you'll come to me."

"I promise... I never..." she began with trembling lips. "Rose has said it well. You will always be in my prayers. Now go, Levi, please. To prolong this parting is only to make it more difficult. May God be with you, and may the north star guide your steps. I'll never forget you..."

With that, she released him and rushed into the building. He watched her disappear with a sinking heart.

Chapter Nineteen

Exactly one week after leaving Aurora and James at the Charity School, Angus showed up at Levi's farm with a Narragansett in tow. Levi was in the barn cleaning out a stall when he recognized the weary and saddened Angus. The horse with an empty saddle brought a frown to his brow. He rushed out to greet Angus.

"I've been expecting you any day now, Angus. I'm relieved to see you arrive home safely." He recognized the horse as belonging to the youngest man in the company — Thomas Ellsworth from Derryfield. "What happened?"

Angus was near tears as he handed the reins to Levi. "It was the strangest thing I've ever seen, Colonel. We had just left Lake Champlain and were following the St. Francis River to Canada when we were jumped by a band of twenty or so renegades. They were well trained and well-armed with rifled carbines much like our own. They hit us on both flanks at the same time with some cavalry and some infantry. They were desperate for supplies and probably any female company they could capture."

"Didn't you have flankers out?" Levi questioned.

"Sure, but they did not pick up anything out of the ordinary. The attack came before my flank runners had reached their attack point. Tom was the right flank rider, and he was killed instantly. The moment it happened, I ordered the wagons to close up and form a perimeter defense line around them. It was the most intense engagement I've ever experienced. They eventually broke off the assault and fled. We had killed or wounded twelve of their men. Tom was our only death. Four men were wounded, two Indians and Robert Stearns and Kent Towle."

"Where are the wounded?" Levi asked with concern.

"I left all of the wounded at the Indian encampment at Odanak. Ranger Bedell was there at the time. He promised to see that justice was done and that our two wounded were escorted home when they were well enough to travel. Bedell has a party of three white men and three Abenaki Indians in his squad of rangers. I brought Tom's belongings to his home in Derryfield. The horse is yours."

Levi grasped his young subordinate and gave him a bear hug. "You've done well, Angus. Your father's spirit must look upon you with great pride. You've been a fine officer and I'm proud to have served with you. Now go home to your family and rest your body and soul. You've earned that. I'll go to see Tom's family tomorrow. I wish I could pay you some of the wages you've earned, but there is no money left in the state's treasury."

"I understand, Sir," Angus replied, with a shrug of his shoulders.

"I have offered a fifty acre piece of land down by the river to a prospective buyer. When it sells, I plan to share it with you and the others. Here, take these gold coins. They are the last ones. Please take them. I'm so ashamed for all of you who have served so faithfully and sacrificed so much. The state has treated you poorly. You deserved better. If you need more, come to me, and I'll figure out some means to help you."

Angus hesitantly accepted the coins. "Thank you, Sir. It has been a privilege to serve with you. Now that I'm here in New Boston, I feel let down a little. I thought homecoming would be an explosion of joy and happiness, but it eludes me, and I'm bothered by that fact."

"I've had the same feelings, Angus. I still find it difficult to adapt to the chores of the farm. It's almost as if something is missing, and I don't know what it is. The trails we've shared will never be forgotten. They can never be understood by the loved ones we left behind either. Our brotherhood of warriors is a distinct group that I'm very proud of. Our transition to the pastel life of farming will take a while for us to adapt, but it will happen, young man." Levi slapped the rump of Angus' horse and waved good-bye.

Late in November, winter finally came to the Wilson farms on the high ridge east of the village of New Boston. Snow two feet thick blanketed the countryside. Levi was prepared for the onslaught of winter and the isolation the deep snow imposed. He and his cousin Malcolm, his closest neighbor, had stacked twenty cords of firewood in the woodshed connecting the house with the barn. The root cellar was filled to capacity with potatoes, squash, apples, turnips, and two barrels of cider. A small amount of dried corn had been ground into meal at the Campbell grist mill run by Angus and his family.

One day in mid-December, Levi was surprised by a postal rider who handed him a letter from Aurora. He sat down to read it beside the kitchen fireplace.

Charity School
Hanover, New Hampshire
December 11, 1781

Dear Levi,

I was fortunate to learn of a rider going to Derryfield who consented to take our letters with him.

You will be pleased to learn that James has adapted to the school beyond our expectations. I'm so proud of his progress. He asks about you often, and I tell him that you must be busy preparing for the long winter ahead.

I have been busy tutoring some students in English and acting as guidance counselor for the younger students. It's exciting to see how eager they are to learn. My efforts are enough to pay for our support, and I'm thankful for the employment, especially for the winter.

I think often about our trip with you. It may be bold of me to write, but I wanted to let you know how well things have worked out for us. Thanks again for helping to make it possible. You have placed us in a new world that I pray will accept us. Our culture has been irreversibly altered by the invasion of the more dominant western civilization. If I were white, I would rejoice, but my racial heritage limits what I will be able to do in your world, and that saddens me.

I apologize for my brooding. Thank you, again, for everything. I hope that this finds you well and content with your life.

Aurora and James

Levi placed the letter on the large table in front of the fireplace. He could still picture her riding straight and proud, thinking only of her grandson. Ever since their parting at Hanover, she had dominated his thoughts. The farm brought back warm recollections of Beth and little Naomi, but they were memories from a distant past that he would always treasure. Aurora had come into his life a total stranger and left, in many ways, still a stranger, yet one whom he felt he had known for a long time. She was a true dilemma. He questioned if he had been too bold expressing his emotions. Collecting pen and ink, he sat down to write an answer to her letter.

New Boston

January 1, 1782

Dear Aurora,

Another year has passed, and, for the first time in my adult life, I'm able to stay here on the farm. The New Hampshire Congress has officially retired our Border Company from service. The New Hampshire Rangers that are now actively functioning in the northern forest with Abenaki assistance have done a marvelous job in bringing the two factions closer together.

I was most pleased to receive your letter and to learn the good news about James. He is a brave young man who has earned a permanent place in my heart. Give him a big hug for me and tell him that I think often about our trip together.

Shortly after I returned home, I traveled to Exeter to settle our affairs with Congress. When that was completed, I spent some time with Daniel and Lavina Cullen. My Lord, he certainly has a broad grasp of affairs of state. Almost daily he receives notices and announcements from all along the Atlantic seaboard. You were correct about the loss of their only son. They are still devastated and find it difficult to talk about him. DC was planning to marry Rose Waters. They had nothing but praise for her and consider her a part of their family. She earned their affection when she and her brother lived with them for a while.

Now, I want to scold you for your remarks about race. I've just visited two of the most loved and respected individuals I've ever known — Daniel and Lavina. Their love for each other has nothing to do with race or cultural heritage and everything to do with feelings from the heart. Trust, respect, honesty, and courage are virtues that transcend all cultures and are universally admired.

I am fifty-five years old, and I've lived two thirds of my life. Time is running out for me, but one thing I can tell you with complete truth — I found you to be a wonderful person whom I liked to be with. When I left you at Hanover, a part of me stayed with you. I hope that I am not making you uncomfortable with these words, for the last thing I want to do is to hurt you who gives so much of yourself to others.

I have bared my true feelings for you to evaluate. Do not make light of them for they come from the heart, and I have never spoken with a forked tongue! If I were younger, I would not be this bold.

Wishing you and James all the best.

Levi

Early the next morning, Levi saddled his favorite Narragansett and posted the letter in the village of New Boston. He spent several days anxiously awaiting a reply from Aurora, regretting that he had declared his feelings for her and concerned that he had been too bold. One cold blustery day in

171

February his cousin knocked on the door to deliver the anticipated letter.

"Hey, Levi, it's me, Malcolm."

Levi placed his quill pen on the worn desk and answered his cousin's call. "Come in, Malcolm. Brrr, it's cold out there today. What have you got?"

"I just passed the post carrier who gave me this packet of mail for you," he explained. "I just received a copy of the COASTAL BEACON with a great story about the large exodus of Loyalists leaving the country for New Brunswick or Nova Scotia. The British have withdrawn from North Carolina, but they still have a large force occupying New York."

Levi glanced at the packet of mail and noted a letter with Aurora's familiar penmanship. "Thanks, Malcolm. Have you got time for a cup of hot tea?"

"Sure. I was up to Carl Holland's place in Weare. He is most happy with the German soldier that surrendered to General Stark at Bennington a few years ago. As a matter of a fact, the German is planning to purchase a large tract of land on the river. Could a former enemy do that?"

Turning his head in a gesture of interest, Levi thought for a moment what his cousin had asked him. "I'm not sure, Malcolm. I know that many of the Hessian soldiers have opted to stay here instead of being shipped back home to Germany. Stark told me that he admired them. They were great soldiers who gave his regiment a tough fight. They came from a mountainous area similar to New Hampshire. As long as he declares his allegiance to our newly established country, I don't see any problem with him owning land like other citizens."

They sat at the large tavern table in front of the blazing fireplace and talked about the things discussed in the newspaper. A large force of 7,000 British soldiers under General Clinton had arrived at Chesapeake Bay. Upon hearing of the surrender of General Cornwallis at Yorktown, they picked up anchor and returned to England. If they had arrived earlier, the outcome of the war would have been different.

"Thank God," Levi vented with relief. "Seven thousand more trained British troops would have swallowed our meager forces."

"Well, Levi, I'll let you get to your mail. You always seem to be busy doing something. I envy your industry, cousin. Thanks for the tea."

"You're welcome," Levi replied, closing the door behind him. He placed another log on the fire and sat down to read Aurora's letter.

Hanover

January 29, 1782

Dear Levi,

Your letter came two days ago. I've given much thought about my response. I am flattered to be the object of your affection and could never treat such honesty lightly.

Your kind words initially made my heart want to sing, but after reflecting on our differences, I had doubts that your feelings might change once you returned home and renewed old friendships.

Our time together was so short, and there are those in your society who would look upon me as an inferior and second-rate, much like the negro slaves. Please don't be angry at my words which only reflect the attitudes of many.

Your kind words gladdened my heart, and I can assure you that those feelings you honestly expressed are reciprocated. I am not a young woman. I once had the love of a fine husband, so I know what two people together can create. I never thought another man could make me feel like that again, but you have succeeded in making it possible by being your gentle self. My heart sings and cries at the same time!

Thank you for being honest with me. I don't know what tomorrow brings, so I'll just be content and happy with the knowledge that I, a Native American of fifty-one years, have won the affection of a fine, courageous soldier. My heart and my vivid imagination do not allow me to take those dreams any further.

You mention in your letter how you feel, but you did not outright declare that you love me. I can say it without hesitation. I love you, Levi Wilson.

Aurora

Spring arrived, turning the cart tracks into rivers of mud that discouraged travel. Levi welcomed the warmer weather, anxious to see how well the two hundred apple and one hundred peach trees had fared over the winter. The hilltop was covered with blossoms. The sight of them in bloom gladdened his heart. He had frequently been away at this time of year. The orchards had been an obsession with his father, who had cleared the land and planted a few trees each year. Now, they were bearing large crops of apples, a staple food for the family.

Levi had completed the pruning of each tree by the end of March when he noticed that he was much more tired than usual. Over the years he had been blessed with a rugged constitution and was rarely sick. Two weeks before, he had visited John Stark in Derryfield who had recently inoculated his entire family and hired help against smallpox. The disease was common throughout the colonies.

One day small red spots developed all over Levi's body. He knew what they meant. He had seen the dreaded smallpox ravage entire companies of soldiers. A few like Stark and General Washington had survived, but most succumbed to the high fevers and bouts of delirium. Malcolm and his wife, Maureen, found Levi lying flat on his back, too weak to move.

The first day he was confined to his bed, one of his cousins, who was a student at Dartmouth College, had received word from Angus to contact Aurora at the Charity School. Three days later, in a driving rain storm, Aurora showed up at the farm riding her horse. Angus was in the woodshed gathering wood for the fireplace when she appeared. The whole neighborhood had been caring for Levi.

Angus embraced Aurora. "My, we are glad to see you."

"How's he doing?" she cried, hoping that she was not too late.

"Come," Angus replied, leading her into the house.

The valiant Levi Wilson, who had survived more violent engagements than most men, was now lying helpless in a delirious state on a cot in the room just off the kitchen. He was bathed in sweat and covered with oozing foul-smelling sores that were extremely contagious to those who cared for him. She removed her coat and kneeled down beside Levi's bed. He was burning up with sweat beads running down his face. She was alarmed at his condition and begged Angus to bring her cold water to help fight the fever that could take his life.

"We've got to bring his fever down as soon as possible," she lamented, kneeling beside his bed. Angus returned with a full bucket of cool spring water and several large linen sheets.

Aurora doused a large sheet in the water pail, then wrapped it under his two armpits and around his head. She wrapped another wet cloth around his chest and stomach and asked for more water. Angus was quick to comply with her request. She liberally sprinkled more water over the cloths keeping them saturated with cool water. Once the cloth began to warm from the fever, she doused it again using up four buckets of water in the first two hours of her presence. She told him to disregard the water spilled on the wide white pine floor boards. It could be cleaned up later. Levi's dangerous condition required all of her attention.

He saw how she went about trying to lower his fever and approved of her timely methods. He was fully aware of her concern for Levi. She was familiar with the ravages of the disease and had no disillusions that most of the time, it ended with death. She prayed that Levi's strong constitution would be able to fight off the disease. The water-soaked cloths were helping to make Levi more relaxed even in his delirious state. Once the cloths were soaked, she treated each pus-filled sore on his face and upper body with soothing witch hazel and flaxseed oil she had brought from Hanover.

Infections from the draining sores was a real threat to Aurora. She washed her hands frequently in strong lye soap. Much of her knowledge of herbs and their treatment of the sick came from her long-time friends, Lavina Cullen and Ruth, both of whom were Ojibwa Indians who had worked throughout the northern frontier several years before.

Aurora stayed with Levi for twenty-four hours, insisting that she was all right and that Angus should return to his home to care for his own family. She promised to rest in between the cooling bath treatments. Concerned that Levi was not taking enough liquids, she frequently lifted his head and tried to force water and a little hard cider into his mouth. He was thirsty and unconsciously swallowed the liquids. That was a positive sign! She was able to give him several cups of water that first night.

A few hours after dark, Aurora heard the clear call of whippoorwills outside the house. Several called a long distance away to one very close to the eaves of the kitchen. They made her smile. Levi had told her how he missed their melancholic calls at about the same time every evening. Simple things in life had pleased him. He knew what they looked like by drawings, but he had never seen one of the birds in real life because of the darkness.

Seeing the strong, vibrant Levi lying so still and helpless moved her. Curled up on the cot in a fetal position made him look smaller and more vulnerable than ever. The disease was a killer of thousands, and she prayed that he would be spared. He had been a major player in countless violent engagements over the years, yet he had escaped physically unscathed. The emotional scars from those engagements most likely would remain with him forever. Now he was at death's door with his strong body fighting for survival against a powerful unseen enemy. "It wasn't fair," she silently cried. A man who had dedicated his life defending the frontier dwellers deserved to live his senior years in an atmosphere of peace and harmony.

That first night she maintained the fire all night long. The wood was dry and heated the kitchen so that it was comfortable. Aurora drank tea throughout her vigil so as to remain alert in case he needed something. She was able to successfully lower his temperature. His brow was not as hot to her touch as it had been when she first arrived. She was making a positive difference, and that raised her spirits.

The rain had stopped, and the sun rose over the twin mountains to the east. Sunshine burst through the two windows in the kitchen, filling the room. Weary and fatigued, Aurora stepped outside to look around and to breathe the fresh morning air. She saw the row upon row of apple and pear trees in the northern fields. Levi had often talked about them with pride. She quickly surveyed the yard, the barn, and the smaller orchard south of the house. There was a feeling of permanency about the well-maintained country home. Now she understood

Levi's longing to be home. There was an aura of peace about the place that comforted her.

She quickly walked into the barn to see if any of the animals needed to be fed or watered. Opening the side door to the barn, she was surprised to see a younger man than Levi cleaning out a horse stall.

"Hello," she announced, approaching the man.

Malcolm was a sturdy, red-headed Scotch-Irishman with an infectious smile. "Hello, you must be the one called Aurora."

"Yes, I came to check on the animals. Levi is resting comfortably now. His breathing is less labored than last night."

Malcolm set aside the shovel in his hand and announced, "I would have dropped by the house, but I was afraid I might wake you up. I'm Levi's cousin, Malcolm. I live in the next house up the road a ways. We are relieved that you could come."

"When I heard that he was ill, I could not stay away," she replied truthfully. "Levi told me about the three Wilson brothers of New Boston."

Malcolm pointed to a stall in the barn. "I placed your horse there and just fed her a good measure of oats. The saddle is on the rail beside the stall."

"Thank you. The horse was a gift from General John Stark in Stillwater, New York."

"We've been worried about Levi. The pox is a horrible disease. We pray that he'll survive." Malcolm looked at her with beseeching eyes. "What is your opinion? Will he be able to fight the cursed disease? He has the reputation of being a fearless fighter. Perhaps he has found a superior combatant in the pox..."

Aurora placed a reassuring hand on Malcolm's arm. "Do not despair. I honestly believe he can successfully fight the disease. At first, his fever was dangerously out of control, but with massive amounts of cool water and the good Lord's help, his fever has lessened. If it had continued much longer, he would have perished. By early morning, I could detect that his fever was coming down. He was more comfortable and was breathing easier. We have that to be thankful for. I join you in praying that we have broken the grip the disease has on your cousin."

Malcolm listened to the modest lady with the soft, reassuring voice. "That's the best news I could hear, dear lady. My cousin, Levi, has been a lonely man ever since his wife, Beth, died. He was not the same after that. For years at a time, he roamed the frontiers without returning home. Home reminded him of his loss, and that tormented him for a long time."

"He mentioned that to me one evening on the trail."

"When he came home this time, he was different. Of course, he was older and had made up his mind to retire from the long trails he had followed for years. He was more relaxed and at ease than any of his family and friends had ever seen him. When he spoke about you, his eyes betrayed what was in his heart, and we were all thankful that he had found someone that gave meaning to his life. Now that I've met you, I can understand how it has transformed him. We all thank you for that."

Pleased at Malcolm's words, Aurora smiled at him with moist eyes. "I thank you for the kind words. If I've brought clarity of purpose and peace to Levi's life, then I am happy, too." She pulled the doeskin shirt exposing her arm and extended it for Malcolm to see. "The color of my skin and the culture I was born to separate us. In many ways we are still strangers. Our brief encounter on the trail is enough to establish us as good friends, and I value that very much. To assume a deeper and more meaningful relationship could be hurtful."

Chapter Twenty

Malcolm followed the logic of this lovely lady with her arm bared for him to examine. He was trying to understand what she was telling him in her clear melodious voice. He and all of the Wilson family had the habit of plain speaking. He countered her statement with carefully chosen words that she would not misunderstand. "Do you think that our family would not accept you because of your race? Has it made a difference in the way Levi perceives you? Is it not true that all of us humans seek to please God and to be worthy of our place in the sun? The differences between the two races is not as great as you think. The difference in culture is not a wide impassable divide. As a matter of fact, two hearts can readily leap high above the abyss without notice. There is much more that unite us than divide us, dear lady."

His simple words brought tears to her eyes. With trembling lips, she asked, "Do you think that Levi loves me?"

"My cousin, Levi, is a very private person who rarely shares his feelings with anyone. I have not heard him say those words, but I've seen a glow of happiness whenever he mentions your name. I'm not betraying any confidence when I tell you that he deserves someone like you to share his life."

She began to weep, holding her head in her two hands. Malcolm had seen what was in her heart and embraced her. "Do not despair, Aurora. If I have offended you, I'm sorry. My cousin is a very special man, admired by many. My honest opinion is that the two of you must listen to your hearts and let them be your guide."

She composed herself with a wistful smile. "I did not intend to bother you with my overactive imagination. You are

179

kind like your cousin. Now I must return to be with him. I rejoice that we've broken the fever."

"We intend to relieve you so that you can rest, Aurora. I'll take over for the balance of the day. Angus offered to take a turn with him, also. So now, dear lady, you rest so that you do not become exhausted. You've worked a miracle with Levi in more ways than one," Malcolm released her and smiled. "He's a lucky man."

For the next four days, Levi received constant care from Aurora, Angus, and Malcolm, sharing shifts about every twelve hours. His condition slowly improved even when his fever returned several times. They responded with cool water baths that quickly counteracted the dangerously high temperatures. On the third day, Levi was strong enough to be propped up in the bed to take some badly needed solid food for nourishment. Aurora fed him oatmeal with liberal amounts of maple syrup, smiling at his legendary sweet tooth which made it easier for them to give him solid food anytime he was alert enough to do so.

When he was sleeping he seemed to be more relaxed. Beads of sweat no longer formed on his brow. It was on that third day that he recognized Aurora. She had whispered in his ear if he wanted to eat something. The room was dark except the light from the fireplace flames.

He recognized her voice. "How long have you been here, Aurora?" he asked in a low voice.

With that question, she was assured that they had nursed him through the worst of the disease. "I came as soon as I heard that you were sick, Levi. You had all of us worried about your condition. The fever has left you weak and dehydrated, so we'll be patient while you get stronger." She swept a strand of hair from his eye and placed her hand on his brow, reassured that he felt normal.

"How long have I been sick?" he asked with a thick tongue.

"About a week. Now you concentrate on resting, Levi."

"I heard your voice, and it was as if I was dreaming," he cried, grasping her hands in his. "You're a remarkable lady."

She leaned over him and kissed him on the forehead. "Thank God you are improving, Levi. I was afraid that I could not save you..." She swiftly wiped away a tear forming in her left eye.

"I love you, Aurora," Levi replied in a weak voice. "I'm sorry if I've been…"

A flush of happiness embraced her. She kissed him again. "Hush, now. You have not been a bother to me. Close your eyes and rest. I will be with you for the rest of the night."

He yielded to her request and closed his eyes, shortly, he was asleep. She felt like shouting to the world that he loved her. Joy filled her heart, and a prayer of thanksgiving softly caressed her lips.

A year later, Levi walked out into the apple orchard filled with blossoms. He stopped to admire the presence of the mountains to the east and reflected on his good fortune. A few months after he recovered from smallpox, he and Aurora were married in the small church in the village. It was a happy occasion enjoyed by the entire community. Those close family members who knew him well saw how the soft-spoken Delaware Indian maiden, Aurora, brought joy and contentment into his life. Little James left the Charity School in Dartmouth for the school in New Boston where he continued to impress his teacher with his academic abilities.

Levi had much in his life to be thankful for, yet when he thought of those courageous individuals who had shared the trails with him and perished in violence, he always had the lingering feeling that if he had done something differently, they might have survived. It was a sobering part of his life that he would take to his grave. He was shaken from his reverie by a voice which always touched his heart.

"Levi," Aurora called, holding a letter in her hand. She was dressed in her traditional doeskin hunting shirt sprinkled with red and blue beads, and her hair fell loose about her shoulders. He thought she was the most beautiful lady in the world, and he loved her dearly for her gentle ways. "The post rider just dropped this off, Levi."

He accepted the letter and broke the wax seal. Aurora placed an arm around his waist as he read the letter aloud:

Continental Army Headquarters
Newburgh, New York
May 15, 1782

Dear Colonel Levi Wilson,

I have just been informed that you successfully overcame the dread disease smallpox. That makes us brothers in a select fraternity who survived the curse. I send you congratulations for that achievement and for your recent marriage to a very special lady who has left a wonderful legacy of sacrifice across the northern frontier.

I must apologize for not acknowledging your thirty years of selfless service to our very young nation. No one served it with greater courage and distinction than you and your small New Hampshire Border Company.

You have left a legacy of devotion to duty beyond compare. Most of your service was rendered beneath the dark canopy of the wilderness where the enemy was often heard but seldom seen. The long desolate trails are now behind you, but they were an important part of bringing a collection of individual states into a single nation.

A grateful nation says thank you, dear friend. May your days be filled with short trails with the wind at your back and the sun on your face. This nation salutes you.

I shall always be your humble and obedient servant.

General George Washington
Commander in Chief, Continental Army

The End

Other Historical Romance Novels
BY
Clifton LaBree

A Song for Lisa   A Historical Romance

This is the story of a young American woman captured by the Japanese in the Philippines, 1941. Like most prisoners, she was brutalized and sadistically treated with a cruel disregard for human life. Three years later, Lisa and her companions had reached the low point of starvation and abuse .....

Lake of Three Sorrows   A Historical Romance

A warm spiritually uplifting story of courage, commitment, and sacrifice. This is the story of Dale Cooper, a battle-weary American soldier who served in two world wars.

Flickering Flame (Colonial Series Book One)

A historical novel, about the Cullen family who settled in Portsmouth, New Hampshire, and their participation in events prior to the French and Indian War. Freedom and opportunity were on the march, but it extracted a heavy price. Frontier settlers were ruthlessly killed and butchered by rampaging Indians lead by French officers and Jesuit priests who frequently incited them to greater levels of inhumanity...

Raising the Torch (Colonial Series Book Two)

A continuation of the saga from Flickering Flame, Colonial Series book one, of the Cullen family in Colonial Portsmouth. This is a moving story of love and sacrifice when a small colony had the audacity to fight for independence from their motherland...

Non-Fiction Books

By

Clifton LaBree

New Hampshire's General John Stark, Live Free or Die: Death Is Not the Greatest of Evils

Publisher - Fading Shadows Imprint

A fresh look at one of America's staunchest defenders of liberty and freedom. John Stark was a courageous New Hampshire citizen-soldier who fought in both, the French and Indian War, and the Revolutionary War. His pursuit of leadership excellence on the battlefield distinguished him as one of the most successful combat commanders of the war, and one of the least appreciated.

His selflessness, modest life style, and devotion to the cause of freedom are an inspiration that time has not diminished. He remains today the embodiment of the frugal, independent, and cantankerous New Hampshire Yankee.

Gentle Warrior, General Oliver Prince Smith, USMC

Published by - Kent State University Press. Kent, Ohio, 2001

The Story of one of the United States Marine Corps best General Officer. His flawless performance in Korea is a story that needed to be told.

FADING SHADOWS IMPRINT

Fading Shadows Imprint was established to bring to the public books of historical events and portraits of people enduring tragic circumstances of by-gone days. Hopefully, they will generate a deep appreciation and respect for the exceptionalness of the United States of America, and an appreciation for the sacrifice and selflessness of those who valiantly served for liberty and freedom.

The characters are fictional, but the historical events and dates have been seriously researched and are factually presented. Some books feature incidents during the French and Indian Wars as well as the War for Independence.

World Wars I and II are eras rich in stories that beg to be told. I've tried to pay tribute to the collective courage and heroism, often unheralded, that has defined Americans in every engagement. It was a time when the immortality of dreams and aspirations were defended by the blood of young men and women. There is a beautiful monument and cemetery in a small French village where thousands of white crosses and Stars-of-David are set in perfect alignment, honoring thousands of American soldiers who gave their last full measure. A large granite slab bearing mute witness to their sacrifice has the following words chiseled in stone: TIME WILL NOT DIM THE GLORY OF THEIR DEEDS. Another monument reads: VIRTUE AND COURAGE ARE THEIR OWN MONUMENT AND REWARD. Those simple words define the American soldier from the dark days of the Revolutionary War to the present. They are an American treasure, unique in the history of the world.

Every generation has its own signature and characteristics that uniquely define them. The World War II generation is defined by the immortality of the ideals and truth they gallantly defended.

The United States has freely given precious blood and treasure to defend the rights of man to be free, and we have never asked for anything in return. No other nation on the planet has sacrificed so much for the noble virtues of liberty and freedom. We hope that the selections offered by Fading Shadows Imprint will touch your hearts and generate a deeper appreciation and love for our country.

www.ingramcontent.com/pod-product-compliance
Lightning Source LLC
Chambersburg PA
CBHW072137170626
46813CB00004BA/1604